THE SWIMMING OF THE DEER

THE SWIMMING OF THE DEER
Barry Stewart Hunter

First published in 2020 by
Martin Firrell Company Limited, 10 Queen Street Place,
London EC4R 1AG, United Kingdom

ISBN 978-1-912622-28-3

Typeset in Baskerville.

For R – with love and squalor

Ah, love, let us be true
To one another! for the world, which seems
To lie before us like a land of dreams,
So various, so beautiful, so new,
Hath really neither joy, nor love, nor light,
Nor certitude, nor peace, nor help for pain;
And we are here as on a darkling plain
Swept with confused alarms of struggle and flight,
Where ignorant armies clash by night.

MATTHEW ARNOLD, *Dover Beach*

And on a sudden, lo! the level lake,
And the long glories of the winter moon.

ALFRED, LORD TENNYSON, *Morte d'Arthur*

PART FIRST
Promises and Lies

CHAPTER ONE
The Mantle of the Lake

THIS WAS IN THE DAYS WHEN I WAS just starting out as a writer – I mean a proper writer, a writer of stories. I had penned some poems, of course – mostly derivative of the love poets I admired from later school classes – and these awkward verses I had submitted from time to time, using an assumed name and gender, to a perfectly respectable literary periodical without success. Then I resolved to branch out stylistically and thematically. In scripting a set of narrative portraits, more or less bitter or spiteful according to personal experience and the changing phases of the moon, of people I knew and didn't yet know in and around our fair village of less than three hundred souls, I understood my method was fundamentally voyeuristic, my motive vindictive. That was, or is, fine by me – to this day I leave sanctity to mendicant monks and those who are easily published. The one exception in all this was young Davy James. When I asked if I might tell his story, warts and all, no holds barred, he saw immediately how to redeem me. That, at any rate, was how I chose to view it on behalf of the two of us, our starving hearts coming together briefly in the keen air beside the solid water. Who's to say I wasn't right in what I felt? An adult osprey hung, wings powerfully extended, in the pillar of sky directly above the frozen lake as we two conversed rapidly, at close range, and with maximum prejudice in the rationed afternoon.

3

What did the cruel bird detect below? In the latest of these muscular and hysterical images I saw the head and neck of a mature whitetail buck taken up totally by the icy grip of the lake, the beast's summer antlers discarded hurriedly on this side or that in a desperate show of surrender. As a vestige of last night's trademark dream the scene was at once familiar and shocking to me. Now the doomed ungulate wore the mantle of the lake at its throat like an enormous aluminium collar, grotesque and dully glittering.

'I don't give a toss what you write,' Davy said, the blood running from his nose still on one side. In concert with his bloodstained shirt and blazer, the miniscule knot of his school tie, impossibly tight and ridiculously poignant it seemed to me, bore grim sartorial witness to his recent struggle with the forces of reaction, so prevalent at home and abroad in those curtained days and shuttered nights. The outsized trousers, borrowed presumably from someone else's chest of drawers and pressed into service at short notice, were belted high above the youth's waist using string. As for his own school trousers – these he carried, I was willing to bet, in the nylon shopping bag he swung back and forth automatically in a metronomic dumb-show of sublimated emotion. 'You can make the whole goddamned thing up as far as I'm concerned,' he went on, planting distressed shoes wider apart on the shingle shore and fixing me with his most defiant stare. 'No one gives a bugger about me anyway.'

He was quite wrong about that last part. There and then I could think of at least one villager prepared to prove it to him, within the limits of a recurring dream at least, in the most unequivocal terms. 'Would you care to borrow my handkerchief?' I asked him rather primly, although I could see the blood was already beginning to set, liquorice-like, on the pale pediment of his upper lip with its smudge of incipient facial hair. There was no sign now above the lake of the rapacious bird of prey. Of the stricken whitetail stag below there was no further intimation.

'What? And ruin it for good?' Davy said with a harsh little laugh, very self-deprecating, as if to suggest his blood was more dangerous or more damaging to a handkerchief than anyone else's, or simply dirtier than all the rest.

'Of course, I can't guarantee to make all of it true,' I said. 'Some of it will have to be imagined, will it not? I mean the parts you can't possibly expect to know about or tell me about, for example, because you weren't actually there. Perhaps I can make it true in spirit –'

We were at that uncertain time of day immediately before the self-absorbed decline or descent – the blind rush towards darkness that hesitates only in the face of the lovely gloaming itself. It was the hour set aside for promises and lies. Then Davy wiped the blood from his lips and spat some of it out and looked at me pityingly. 'You don't have to make it true,' he said, eyes narrowing with renewed hostility or distaste. 'Just make it hurt.'

CHAPTER TWO

Best Country in the World

WHERE DOES IT BEGIN? IT BEGINS IN THIS special place – a place of immortal hills and flashing streams and lakes full of fishes. When does it begin? It begins today in a harsh, harsh winter – the coldest winter, Adam Boyd says, for fifteen years. The last time it was this cold, Davy was arse-down in a cot, waving his tootsies in the air and balling his eyes out. A great deal can change in the space of fifteen winters – too bloody right it can. Old man Murphy flogs his prime land to some ponce in a sheepskin jacket come all the way up here from bloody Leeds or Sheffield, and before you know it the fields are cordoned off by men in white coats bearing clipboards and ballpoint pens. The bulldozers will be up here next, Adam Boyd argues, for to tear down our trees and make our hills flatter. This year's will be the last Scramble, he says, before our hill is taken away for good. See if I'm not right. The last chariot race is just over the horizon, Adam insists prophetically or apocalyptically, although his indifference to the annual spectacle is well known locally. Everything changes, but everything stays the same. That is all right. That is axiomatic. This is our country – the best country in the world.

There is an old stone house, noble but austere, on the northern shore of the lake. To all intents and purposes, it is exactly the same house as it has always been. While the front of the building harvests

6

the seasonal sunlight patiently, never greedily, and with a stoical air, the two little bedrooms shiver at the sides of the house on the upper floor. These two humble rooms won't really warm up until August, if they warm up at all. It depends, does it not? It all depends. This is the house in which Davy James, fifteen and a half years of age at the latest count, lives with his mother, Lydia, a well-made woman who, although scarcely in the first flush of youth, is still attractive in a half-forgotten way, and who drinks each night and every day of the week, not excepting Sundays. There are just the two of them existing side by side in this cold stone house on the northern fringes of the lake, a state of domestic affairs which has always obtained, and which will presumably continue to do so because, in the absence of the major revelation or shock, everything stays the same in these parts.

There is no school today. It gets dark so early at this time of the year. The old house is full of shadows cast by a solitary street light on the little road which describes the margins of the lake at this point, and which circles back in its own time and at its own speed to the loose aggregation of homes, shops, churches, hotels, farms and outhouses that make up our village on the lake's southern shore. Davy mounts the dozen or so stairs inside the house carefully and deliberately, his heartbeat quickening from one second to the next. That the youth's self-awareness is at its most acute right here and now, at the moment of no returning, is natural enough. The mother is not at home – that is important to bear in mind. The son might just as well be climbing a stairway to heaven or the steps of a scaffold – that is how it presents itself to him, this ritualistic ascent, which he makes again today for a good reason, a private reason.

At the top of the stairs is a narrow landing with, to left and right, the two modest bedrooms of the house. Davy goes first into his own

7

bedroom – here he undresses hurriedly as far as his underpants and socks. He doesn't feel cold at this time. In fact, his armpits are damp and his skin is on fire as usual. Everything is going rather well today. Everything is going according to plan. Glinting provocatively among the shoes and the shadows at the bottom of the wardrobe is a Charles Atlas chest expander. Davy scoops the contraption up in one supple movement, carries it through to his mother's room, and lays it out like a body of surgical instruments on the floorboards in front of the dressing table. The next bit is the bit he likes most and least – the bit that really matters or counts, it seems to Davy. (If anyone else were watching they would probably agree with this assessment.) Selecting a summer skirt having an attractive floral motif from his mother's wardrobe he steps into it ably, zips it up deftly, and twists it around so that the short zipper is to the rear. Chosen today more or less at random, this pretty garment is nonetheless one that Davy has worn before. Of course, he permits himself no favourites as such from the rack. At least he tries not to. That would be going too far.

Now he is ready. If he squats just a little, he can see his reflection in the mirror of the dressing table. Arms straining, bare breast puffed up with air, Davy holds his chest expander like an accordion of metal springs in front of, and close to, his torso. He stretches the squeaking apparatus to one side and the other as far and as hard as he can, but his face remains a mask. How pretty the pattern of this skirt would look in bright sunlight, the youth thinks. He can't remember seeing it in those circumstances – not ever. Meanwhile, his contraption is still at full stretch. With any luck his biceps will start to twitch soon, for that is always a good sign. No time – from below comes the sound of the front door opening and closing. Davy hears his mother call his name once, twice, from the bottom of the stairs. Released, rejected, the Charles Atlas chest expander hits the floorboards with a complex clattering noise quite unlike any other noise in the physical universe. As he scrabbles at the zipper of his mother's skirt, Davy pants finally from his disciplined exertions. And yet everything is all right here. A pail in the corner of the room catches the drops of rainwater falling every twenty seconds or so from the ceiling and, from beyond that, the leaking roof. Certain empty bottles congregate on the floor of the mother's wardrobe, as they very often will. The clothes rail of the wardrobe is hung tightly enough with dresses and coats, many inside polythene covers. Davy will just have to return the pretty skirt to its rightful place tomorrow, that's all. There is little obvious danger in this. The ice of the lake is two inches thick in places, and summer is so far off. No, the only challenge is a more immediate one – how to cross the upstairs landing from bedroom to bedroom in underpants and socks without being seen from below. But this too is OK.

'Davy, darling – are you all right up there? I heard the most awful clattering sound just now. And why is the house always in darkness, for goodness sake?'

'Everything's fine, Ma. I'll be down in two shakes of a duck's tail. Switch on the lights, why don't you? The lights at the Christmas tree, I mean –'

Now she will be taking off her cloche hat and gloves, the hat in particular wet through from the spiteful showers. Next she will bend down to examine the coal bucket – the bucket Davy already knows is near empty, with precious little fuel to be had at this time from the bunker at the back of the house. Soon she will strike a match to light one of several paraffin stoves that are increasingly their chief mode of heating upstairs and downstairs. Then she will lift the padded lid of the stool in front of the upright piano and deposit there the bottle and bible taken from her handbag. Now the radiogram with its offer of spiritual comfort is in her sights, but she looks likely to disdain it.

9

And, ultimately, yes, she will illuminate the small Christmas tree in the bay window and draw the curtains more closely around it as he descends in a great rush to judge her silently all over again with his terrible patience and understanding.

Everything is as it should be. He is wearing his own clobber again. He has his shoes on now. He is running hell for leather down these stairs. On the threshold of the evening, or the night, he pauses just long enough to pull the front door closed violently behind him. Now he is in a narrow enclosure between house and road, a slice of garden that is home to two bicycles, with the light of the street lamp on his back. He hears a knocking from the bay window as he jerks free a heavy pram wedged between the side of the house and the wall of stones that has seen better days. She is there at the window beside the Christmas tree – of course she is. But Davy cannot look at her. Not now. It wouldn't be right. Instead he heaves three big rocks from the tumbledown wall into his enormous perambulator and squeezes the ugly thing through an open gate hanging crookedly on one hinge and suddenly he is free. In fact, he is free up to and including a certain point that varies with the level of his self-possession, the barometric pressure currently in play, and the action of the spheres on the liquid content of his body, among other factors. Since he is preternaturally aware of next to everything at this moment, Davy is quite conscious of the limitations on his personal freedom.

No moon and no stars – just the cold rain that seems to arrive from every direction at once. On the desolate road that hugs the lake on its way to the village he meets no one and nothing. He sees nothing and no one. For a mile and three-quarters there is just Davy and the big pram, running and rolling together as one machine, rolling and running together as a team. And after you wind the machine up it practically runs itself. On the flat, that is – always on the flat. Once you attain a type of cruising speed the chariot pulls you along sweetly enough behind it.

Now we are in the middle of the village. The closed shops are in darkness. The wet streets are empty except for a few villagers making their way to or from evensong in silent couples. Standing on a ladder outside the deserted picture house, Adam Boyd fixes the letter Z to a title board above the doors. Then he turns the letter on its side to form an N, the last of the characters announcing next week's feature presentation, which will be A Place in the Sun. When the frenzied charioteer rushes past dangerously close to his ladder, Adam ignores him and his battle cry of *Geronimo-o-o-o*. After all, the gamekeeper's indifference in respect of the Scramble is well documented locally. But for Davy it's a big disappointment. Not to be acknowledged by Adam Boyd is a serious setback for the youth. The sting of it lingers as from a slap in the face long after he leaves the village behind and begins to climb the famous hill. If he can just get to his usual marker and a little bit beyond – then he is on track. Then he is on schedule. To be on course – that is what actually matters in this world and this game. Davy is not crying as such – that would be absurd. He is spent – yes, this much is true. And so, he gives up. He throws in the towel. As he pivots back towards the lake, he glimpses for an outstanding moment the old stone house on its northern shore. Downwards and downwards he plummets. Now the freighted pram drags him faster through the puddles and the potholes until he falls and releases, his breath coming in rasping sobs now. He is flat on his back on a muddy hillside road. He rails at unseen stars. They are up there somewhere, those selfish bastards. They must be keeping their powder dry. What for, though? Why not advertise? If not now, when? Davy is laughing.

He all but giggles for a brief period before he rolls over and vomits sparingly into the dirt. *Geronimo is tight with me* he whispers, eyes lit up from inside. A short distance below him on the slope, the pram rests on its flank like modern art, stones disgorged, two wheels turning.

CHAPTER THREE
Chicken Soup

WHAT A DIFFERENCE A DAY MAKES. The rain has moved eastwards overnight, and now the sky is an untrammelled blue. Reflections of the hills dive deep into the icy lake on one side, never to resurface, while tendrils of smoke climb vertically from two or three chimneys scattered around and above the shore. No smoke rises as yet from a particular chimney, the one in question.

Dressed for school, and singing The Holly And The Ivy without joy or ambition, a youth sweeps the hearth with a little brush plucked from a suite of tools made for just such fireside interventions. Davy is not thinking about the carol he sings. He is not thinking about the routine household duty he discharges. In fact, he is thinking of Adam Boyd, as he so often does. In his mind's eye he pictures Adam in the act of shaving, cut-throat razor held at safe distance as the arms of a woman encircle his bare upper body from behind. What else? There is a shotgun – no, more likely a hunting rifle – leaning idly at the edge of vision. Davy has no idea where this image comes from. He has no proper sense of the identity of the woman – it might be Victoria or Rachel or several others he could probably name if he had to – as she toys with a locket dangling from a cord around Adam's neck. Is it the remnant of a dream, this image? Davy doesn't know. He only knows there is something missing from the scene. Then it comes to

13

him – there is no mirror in the image. Does it matter? Does it matter that something is missing from, rather than present in, a runaway dream? Again, Davy doesn't know. He only knows that the absence of a mirror in a dreamscape is somehow his fault.

There is loud singing now in the room. As he sings, Davy's voice leap-frogs scornfully from falsetto to mock bass and back again as if looking for a place to hide, or to lose itself, or to die. Although Davy James sings loudly enough this morning, his heart is not in it, for this very day he is resolved to confront the whole business – this whole question of the music – with a view to moving things forward in the mindset of his mother. At the precise moment he thinks about his mother she is seated, ninety per cent ready for work, at her dressing table, the upstairs dressing table Davy knows so well, and piling her hair up in a sort of glamour pose for the benefit of her reflection in the mirror. What on earth can she be thinking of? It is true that on the dresser in front of her is a magazine with, on its black and white cover, a Hollywood starlet known to many of us. Perhaps that is the driver of Lydia's mood – certainly she is not normally given to flights of fancy. As part of this demeanour, or for some other reason bound up with her feelings about herself, she has a lighted cigarette hanging from her lips. As the smoke from her cigarette climbs, Lydia squints – now she is practically obliged to map the surface of her dresser in selective detail, finding there in addition to the magazine just noted a mother-of-pearl jewellery box, exquisite and exotic and somehow out of place in this unrelentingly downbeat context, plus a framed photograph of an officer in uniform, or what looks like an officer in dress uniform, its protective glass cracked at one corner. Of course, there are sundry other items on Lydia's dressing table, but she passes over these quite naturally because she understands they hold no real value or interest. Now she does two or three things very quickly, or in quick succession, as though she recognises the time for talking is over. First, she snatches the cigarette from her lips and, having failed to locate a receptacle in which to extinguish it at hand, tosses it into a nearby pail, the pail whose principal job is to catch various droplets falling from above when the need arises, where it goes out with an admonishing hiss. Next she turns the framed photograph face down on the surface in front of her – doubtless she wants to be alone with her thoughts in order to gather them for a new day. Then she opens a drawer and takes a leather-bound hip flask from inside and places the flask on the dressing table and regards it. At around this time she hears loud singing from below and for a wild moment she is her old self again. Yes, she is happy.

In the downstairs room the singing has stopped. Now the radio is on – a BBC newsreader is talking about Egypt, about Suez. These days the news is mostly about troop withdrawals, or the burning of British and French flags. There is often a burning of flags to contend with, Davy decides, in situations like this. As he kneels close to the fireplace he continues to roll up the pages of an old newspaper – soon he will tie these in a kind of loose knot to make a bed for their next fire. Now the wireless falls silent abruptly. The youth turns with a start.

'No need to stand to attention, Davy,' his mother says, regretting this mean-spirited interjection instantly as her son sinks back down again to work on his newspaper strips. 'I'm sorry,' Lydia goes on. 'I barely see you from one day to another, that's all. Switch it on again, by all means, if you want to.'

'Nowt to do with us anyway,' Davy indicates brightly. 'Hungary and Egypt. They could drop an atom bomb on us here and no one would even notice.'

'Perhaps they will one day,' Lydia says in a new, interested voice.

'Will what?' Davy says, dressing the fireplace now with his coils of knotted newspaper. 'Drop an atom bomb, or notice?'

'Davy, darling?' Lydia offers tentatively, as if to branch out in a different direction.

'I know,' the youth says.

'The roof is leaking again,' she tells him anyway.

'That'll be the rain doing what comes naturally to it, I expect.'

'Oh, Davy –' she chides, pulling on her gloves.

'Not me this time, thanks, Ma –' Now he is icing his newspaper cake with little sticks soaked in paraffin. 'It needs proper sorting this time. It needs money. It needs brass.'

'I know that, darling,' Lydia concedes, belting her coat. As she picks up her handbag and turns towards the door, she sees the lights of the Christmas tree are back on. 'Turn the lights off, please, when you leave.' She hears him place his first lump of coal on the sticks in the grate. Soon she has her hand on the doorknob, half in and half out of their world, a world at once fixed, or signed off, and provisory.

'How much are my music lessons?' he asks her. Now he has gone and done it. Now he has challenged her to put a price on her feelings for him, or his for her. He doesn't care about the lessons – not really. In his mind the whole business of the lessons is bound up at any given moment with something much larger – the question of who is paying his school fees from term to term.

'No,' she says firmly after a short pause. She refers, of course, to the music lessons. At the same time, she is thinking – don't question me again about the school fees, please, because everything is taken care of in that regard and there is no need to worry on that account.

'In that case there's always Adam with his famous ladder,' Davy reminds her, as if she needs any reminding. 'Shall I ask him to take a look up there when I see him? I could ask him today if you like.'

'Forget Adam, why don't you? Haven't I said that before?' Is it a warning? Of course it is – a warning to her. How can she tell Davy that Adam is his father? How can she tell Adam that Davy is his son? What good would it do now? Yet with each passing minute the stakes go up. This lie she lives every day – it used to seem almost righteous. It harmed no one – no one, that is, except her. How could she have waited this long? She hears them ask her that question, so pertinent and germane, whenever she looks at the framed photograph on her dressing table. Sometimes they are alone when they ask it. At other times they are together, Adam with Davy. When she sees them side by side like that, she cannot but ask herself – are they more alike, or less? And this is far from an idle game she plays. As each day passes the screw continues to turn inside her. But what galls her right now, faced as she is with a novel consequence of the historic lie, is the idea that allowing Davy to invite Adam Boyd to mend the roof would be the most sensible course of action. Of course it would be – anyone of sound mind can see that. Yet Lydia doesn't want to go there. She can't. If there existed a desert or an ocean between here and Adam Boyd's caravan it wouldn't be enough to separate the past from the present. As for the future – Lydia has never permitted herself to see it as a feasible concept. What possible good would that do? 'Haven't I told you to leave Adam be?' she asks Davy now, her voice trailing off hopelessly the way he hates.

'Why should I, Ma?' he takes up as reasonably as he can. 'Adam Boyd and I happen to be good friends. I mean – he talks to me. He tells me things. Interesting things. Useful things.'

'And I don't?' she says, her forehead pressed hard against the edge of the door.

'You fall asleep with your mouth wide open and your lipstick all over your face. That's what you do.'

At this she takes her forehead from the door and nods slowly. 'There's chicken soup,' she announces although it is early and Davy has school. Again, she cannot quite see why she has used the words she has used. They make no sense under the circumstances. Perhaps they don't need to, she tells herself. As a mother – no, a single parent – she cannot afford to lose heart altogether, she reminds herself. All this takes place rapidly inside her head. 'It's there if you want it,' she calls out, satisfied finally that she has given as faithful an account of herself here as possible. She has made chicken soup. And, after all, this is a small triumph of free will. Emboldened in a modest degree, Lydia steps outside to confront a new day, a day whose astonishing beauty worn so easily and unaffectedly is actually painful to her in the way of a rebuke. Deep down she distrusts such beauty, certain as it is to betray her. She has her bicycle, of course, as does Davy. But the day being so uncommonly fine she elects to walk. Although the mother and the son have virtually the same destination this morning, indeed most mornings during school term, they will make their way to the village separately and under their own steam, single file, two corners apart spiritually at any time, without quite knowing why it should be so. There is nothing remarkable or untoward about that.

CHAPTER FOUR
The Hour of Utmost Uncertainty

PEDALLING HARD ALONG THE QUIET lakeside road, low sunshine picking him out now and then as he rounds this or that bend, Davy has a fixed idea of what he needs to accomplish in the short time left to him before school. His key appointment, a meeting with Adam Boyd, has been scheduled in his imagination pretty much since he finished his fire in the grate. A second encounter, this one with Mrs Lees, will be more of a chance affair. After that – who knows? The day is set fair. Only good can come of such a day, Davy thinks, beset nonetheless by a sense that he has wronged his mother in word.

The rusting caravan that Adam calls home rests on thick blocks of hardwood at the edge of a grassy clearing belonging to the nearby Abercrombie Hotel, a substantial hostelry set in impressive grounds not far from the lake in the heart of the village. As he approaches the site, wheeling his bike along a rutted track of frozen mud, Davy can see the caravan's door is closed. In summer the door is left open, by and large, during the day – to find it closed throughout the winter months is unsettling to the youth in a way he cannot quite get used to. Now he slings his satchel over his shoulder, lowers his bike to the ground, mounts the few steps beside the clapped-out generators and a power cable that runs from the hotel to the caravan's window, and bangs on the door with the flat of his hand. No response.

'It's Davy,' he calls out, backing down one step. No answer. The net curtain at the window gives nothing away. From behind the door comes the voice of a woman. But which woman can it be?

'He's across at the hotel,' Rachel announces from the doorway, rubbing her upper arms in protest at the morning chill and smiling down at the schoolboy in her pleasant, open way. With a toss of her head she sends red hair tumbling luxuriantly around her shoulders. She wears a man's coat – Adam's coat – as a dressing gown. Below the hem of the coat, her feet and ankles are bare. Whoever she is she must be twenty-one or so, Davy decides quickly. For some reason he is compelled to assign an age to anyone and everyone he meets these days. What he is most aware of right now is the contrast in colour, form, texture and tone between this young woman's perfectly made feet and his own shabby shoes. Look – there is even a slice of sock showing through a rent between sole and upper in his right shoe, the shoe he calls on most, presumably, for booting a football against the playground wall and such like.

'Oh,' he says. 'Thanks.' Is that it? Is that all there is, or will ever be, to this encounter? Surely there must be more, Davy tells himself. There must be more to everything under the sun and the moon and the stars. And she agrees. She shrugs now as if to say she can't think of anything meaningful to add. In a flash he resents her. It must be about the split shoe. No, much more likely to concern the milk white breasts he can see riding up amply above the tightly folded arms. 'I thought we'd seen the last of you,' he blurts out finally.

'Oh, Davy,' she says, amused enough to laugh out loud. 'I think what you mean is – I wasn't sure if we'd ever see you again, Rachel.' Here, she draws a cigarette from a pack she extracts like a magician, or a magician's beautiful and talented assistant, from the pocket of her heavy coat and, yes, there is even a book of matches in the other

20

pocket exactly as there should be in life. 'Isn't that what you meant to say this morning?'

At least he knows who she is now. She offers him a cigarette, her last, but he looks away towards the hotel clearly visible between and beyond two giant monkey puzzle trees, their leaves so green as to be practically black in the blue, blue day. He is waiting for her to flirt with him. He is waiting for her to tease him, or to make fun of him. How else could this possibly end? But that is OK with him because it is important, he knows, to practise these situations forever.

'Still at school, Davy?' she asks before blowing a smoke ring into the pristine air just above his head, where it floats briefly like a halo before ascending into heaven.

'Actually, I'm wearing fancy dress for a party that's likely to get underway very soon.'

'Got a girl yet, funny man? If not, I could come to the party with you —'

Rachel is gorgeous. But the thing is this — he hasn't even had his main meeting of the morning yet and already he feels undermined somehow, on the defensive. Is it too late to begin again? Is it too late to run the day all over again from the top? On the first tier of the terraced lawn that descends crisply from the hotel's front towards the lake stands a solitary spruce — here it is that Davy discovers Adam and his trusty ladder, the gamekeeper-cum-handyman in the act of draping coloured light bulbs on a long flex from branch to branch around the handsome tree. It falls to Davy James to feed successive lengths of cable upwards from a large quantity of the material piled in a coil at the base of Adam's ladder, and to be thus engaged in the supply of power to the Abercrombie Hotel's exterior Christmas tree lights, a display much remarked on at this time of year being visible over surprising distance between sunset and midnight, is a municipal responsibility the youth takes seriously enough. If only he had more time on his hands this morning and fewer things on his mind.

'She probably misses my father,' he tells Adam Boyd, returning casually to the subject of his Ma following a lull in their exchange. 'She talks to him sometimes – I mean when she's out of it completely. I can hear her talking to his picture in her bedroom.'

'Your mother's a lush,' Adam says matter-of-factly, disembodied voice descending from the middle branches of the spruce.

'In that case she's a lush with no money to mend our roof.'

'I dare say you're not wrong,' Adam goes on, non-committal, as he climbs down the ladder. 'She used to be a proper beauty, too. Did you know that, Davy?'

'Will you come and look at the roof?' There – he has done what he came here to do, these few words issued less as a question than a statement of what must rightfully happen.

'There's the thing,' Adam takes up, as neutral as hell, or playing for time, or simply not interested one way or the other. 'I'm not sure that's the answer.'

'What is the answer, then?'

'She's that far gone, so she is. She needs someone in her life. And I'm not talking about you.'

For a lively moment Davy considers these three short statements in telling conjunction one with another. 'You don't even call round any more,' he says at last, as if this might point a way forward.

'I have things to do,' Adam says. 'People to see –'

'People to do, you mean, don't you? Like Rachel, for example.' He sails close to the wind because, at heart, he is angry and hurt on account of Adam's apparent indifference. Is he not doing the correct thing here? He is doing the right thing by his mother who is a famous lush. What he wants now is Adam's approval, a thing he has mostly taken for granted from day to day and season to season. Could it be that something has changed, or is changing in front of his eyes? But here comes Müller, the genial and fat German who runs the hotel, beaming as ever and striding across the lawn to check on the status of his justly celebrated Christmas lights.

'Adam, Adam – he is always up a ladder. Isn't it so, Davy? And how is Frau James?'

'I thought we were friends,' Davy says as soon as he is alone with Adam again. 'I thought we were tight, me and you.'

'You're still a boy, Davy.'

'What's that got to do with it? I'm not sure it's even true, is it?'

'There's plenty of time. You've got your whole life ahead of you.'

Time for what, exactly? Time to change – to become a different, as in a better, person? There they go – the little clinchers, the loaded platitudes which say nothing helpful but which speak volumes in the disappointment stakes. Why is Adam Boyd disappointed? Why is he distancing himself on this particular day, if that is indeed what he is doing here? What does he see inside Davy's black heart if not the secret things that no one must know about? In the disowning of Davy James is this a significant moment, a turning point? The youth thinks it is. That is why he lashes out now so immoderately.

'I'm going to win the Scramble, Adam.'

'Oh, aye? If you say so, son. I won't be stopping you –'

'You don't believe me, do you?' What Davy means, of course, is something slightly different. What he means is more like – you don't believe *in* me, do you? And now he must dash. In the hour of utmost uncertainty, he really must fly. Although the youth is discouraged to a considerable extent, he scoops up first his satchel then his bicycle and runs strongly – bravely, even – towards the road. At the massive gates he stops and turns and, yes, Adam is still watching him from the shadow of the exceptional spruce. And, after all, a man is not a monster. A man is only human. Soon they ring out across the lawn and around the lake and from hill to eternal hill above the village – the three words that make everything all right.

'I believe you,' Adam calls out as the lovely lights come on in the branches above him.

He is certain to be late for school. He hates that. In the village streets he is running, weaving his bicycle through morning shoppers with their wicker baskets on their arms, and delivery boys stacking their cardboard boxes and paper parcels on the pavement. Up ahead he spies matronly Mrs Lees pushing a large pram determinedly towards him – she bears down on him rapidly so that he feels it necessary to cross the road in order to avoid her. This defensive action, which he recognises as cowardly and without merit generally, is cut short by her friendly cry. 'Stop that choirboy!' Then, after he has joined her finally with sheepish aspect and a wan smile of acknowledgement or apology, she goes on conventionally enough. 'Good heavens, Davy – I'm not such an old dragon, am I?'

'I'm very sorry,' he assures her straight off, 'about last night.' As a matter of fact, this is an accurate and genuine summary of how he feels about letting the choir mistress down. 'I'm right sorry –'

'We missed you, young man. Again.'

'My voice is breaking, see.'

'Oh, dear – as bad as all that, is it?' Mrs Lees says in her kindly way. 'I think we all know your voice began to head south quite some time ago, do we not?' Here, she nods indulgently at nothing and no one, certain of her congenital rightness. 'But you still *sing*, don't you?' she enquires of Davy conspiratorially. 'Treble, alto, tenor or bass – do you suppose God gives a monkey's which pew you occupy?'

'No, Mrs Lees.' As he says this, he surveys the inside of her pram. Now he is clocking the contents of her pram, a pram unaccountably strewn with assorted banknotes and coins of the realm in many sizes, hues and denominations.

'The last Scramble,' she says by way of explanation. 'Everyone's been bending over backwards to try and make it a bit special.'

At this Davy reaches into his trouser pocket, a pocket that holds, to the best of his knowledge, a single shiny sixpence.

'Oh, no,' Mrs Lees insists quickly, casting a weather eye around the street scene and drawing the youth closer before scooping a five pound note from the floor of the pram and pressing it into his palm. 'Not you, Davy James.'

'We don't need hand-outs, Mrs Lees.'

'I know that, dear,' she says, tapping her lips meaningfully with her forefinger before making briskly off with her mobile repository of public funds.

Naturally, Davy is stunned and not a little resentful. But time is short, and there is more to come in the way of distraction before he can enter the school classroom. At the Post Office, his mother's place of work, the sign in the window of the door reads CLOSED. That is because the manager, a bald man in a grey coat, is remonstrating in an animated way with Lydia James, who must have done something to displease him, while Betty, Lydia's plucky co-worker behind the counter, looks on in helpless frustration, unable as she is to offer any comfort just yet to her colleague. Davy bangs angrily on the shop's glass front with both fists, the one fist deprived of righteous clout by the banknote lurking shamefully within. Beyond the glass the heated protestations come abruptly to an end. The manager vanishes into a back room while Betty consoles Lydia and shoos Davy away with a gesture of the hand from the rear of the shop.

He is very late now. He is very late, but he no longer cares. Inside the bank the dark wood gleams and the tone is hushed, reverential. Davy James, his banknote brazenly in hand now, approaches a male teller with brilliantined hair who wears half-moon spectacles low on the nose. That Davy doesn't know this man is of little or no moment. And although we are clearly inside a banking hall, Davy's banknote is not central to what occurs. The crumpled five quid note will not feature here in a supporting role – as an unlikely bribe, perhaps, or a deposit on a new savings account. In fact, the banknote is the child of happenstance, or an accident of history, or a type of red herring – its latent function is as a marker for hunger or desire.

'I'm afraid we don't open until ten o'clock,' the teller says in a voice suitable for children.

'Is Mr Saunders in, please?' Davy asks without knowing quite how he got to this place.

'And do you have an appointment to see our busy and esteemed manager?'

Here, Davy turns to consult a vast clock that looks down on the banking hall from great height. The schoolboy and the bank clerk – all of us, in fact – can see that the time is currently a smidgeon after nine twenty-five. Now the youth confronts the grille and nods at the condescending teller whose age he puts at fifty. 'As a matter of fact, I do have an appointment,' Davy says. 'For half-nine this morning.'

CHAPTER FIVE
Bethlehem

HAVING KNOCKED AND THEN ENTERED in one decisive movement Davy stands, a little out of breath, at the back of the classroom and awaits his fate. In point of fact he waits to be allowed to sit down at a desk, any desk, with or without a rebuke, sarcastic or witty or clever depending on the alignment of the planets, from the other end of the room where Mr Aldridge, Oxford, approximately twenty-five years of age, attaches a political map of the world to a blackboard. The venerable map, mostly pink in colour and imperial in outlook, puts up an unexpected fight, and for a long moment all eyes are on the latecomer at the back of the classroom – all, that is, except the ones belonging to the foppish history man who, hampered by a shortage of drawing pins, remains focused on the task in hand.

'What is it this time, Davy?' There is nothing remotely clever or funny in this – instead the teacher's enquiry, tossed over his shoulder rather, betokens a genuine curiosity about the lives of others, and a proper interest in making such lives accountable at the earliest age.

'Very sorry, sir.' Again, he apologises – and for what exactly? 'I slept in, that's all.'

'Come on, young man. You can do better than that, can't you? Shall we see if we can jog your memory? Didn't our Erica spot you lurking outside a high street clearing bank not half an hour ago?'

There ensues a period of juvenile banter more or less licensed by the teacher in the interests of classroom democracy and the wider learning experience. To Davy, subject and object of today's hostile attention, such an exchange is the price to be paid for being late.

'He's only gone and robbed the bank, Mr Aldridge,' offers Ted Matthews with mock incredulity. 'That's how skint his mother is.'

'Turn out his pockets,' urges Murdo McLean, rubbing his mitts and licking his cracked lips metaphorically. 'Davy's just rolled your old man, Zibby,' he adds, which silly remark he directs at the bank manager's tomboy daughter. 'He must be having his period, sir. It makes him right confused, so it does.'

'Are you what we call mentally handicapped, McLean?' Zibby Saunders interposes coolly and with a closely calculated concern for Murdo's wellbeing. 'Or just educationally sub-normal?'

'Grow up, Murdo. Sit down, Davy. We were just discussing our little adventure in the eastern Mediterranean, were we not?' Here, Aldridge, having successfully located his map in the space dedicated to it, stabs at its middle parts with a wooden pointer. 'So, Davy – did we get a bloody nose at Suez?'

He is miles away from the Suez Canal. He is miles away from it all. He has had to squeeze his frame onto the end of the bench at a long, shared desk – now everyone else moves up as far as possible in order to isolate him physically. What is it they hate so much? Is it something you can see or touch or smell? Or is it something buried deep inside that is nonetheless visible to those who know where to look? Davy knows the answer – of course he knows. He is one step ahead of them at all times. In any room he is the smartest among the sycophants and the spies. He has to believe that. Is he not the friend of gamekeepers and bank managers and, just possibly, the daughters of said bank managers? And did we get a bloody nose at Suez? Davy thinks he knows the answer to that one, too. In his mind's eye he sees the yellowish skies over Upper Egypt. In his imagination these skies are filled with men hanging under ripped parachutes above the rank canal. Although many of these men are not much older than he is, he is unworthy to be one of them. They are men not unlike Aldridge, presumably, and some of them are already drifting dangerously off course in the crowded skies above the marvellous feat of navigational engineering beside the desert.

'I think our power and influence are declining, sir.' He wants to be liked by the teacher, doesn't he? Logic and proportion – these are the fundamental qualities that teachers look for in a mature student, especially a student who is late for class. 'The real power today lies with Russia and America. Some people in this country are living in the past, that's all.'

Now a hand shoots up. 'Colonel Nasser is a communist, sir.' This insight comes from Erica.

'I agree with Davy,' Zibby Saunders announces calmly. Has she really said it? Did she really say that? There can be no doubt about it now – she is *for him*. 'Britain's future is increasingly in the hands of the United States, sir. Plus, of course, they have Elvis Presley.'

There is a sort of psychological or emotional shockwave running around the room – it emanates from Davy's heart. That someone should take his side, or stand up for him like that, is unprecedented. He wants to hug Zibby, but that would be ridiculous.

'Would you care to expatiate, Elizabeth?' asks Aldridge, passing his pointer from one hand to the other.

'Expatiate, sir?'

'Enlarge, Zibby. Elucidate. Expand our inner horizons.'

'Please, sir?' Murdo says in the voice of an innocent. 'Will you be wanting me to expand your inner horizons at all?'

Now the pointer lands harshly on a hardback book – a study of the Zulu War or the Boer Wars – at the front of the class. A couple of things happen quickly in the interested silence that follows. First, Murdo turns to Zibby behind him and laps the air with his tongue for her benefit alone. Then the classroom door opens with barely a knock to admit the head teacher, an ambitious woman who believes passionately in educating girls and boys alongside each other, and a much younger man, slight in general outline, who walks with a limp as he enters the room behind her.

'So sorry to disturb,' says Miss Montgomery. 'As we know, many of you will be taking Latin from next year, so it's my great pleasure to introduce Mr Darling, who will teach Latin here within our fifth form co-ed programme when the new term begins after Christmas. Of course, some of you will already know Mr Darling, who taught until comparatively recently at good old St Saviour's, over the hill and not so far away.'

There it is. There is no more to the introductions than that. The interlopers exit the room as they entered it – one behind the other. And it seems to the surprised class on the threshold of the Christmas holiday that Mr Darling's limp is really quite pronounced. Is the new master perhaps injured on the rugby field? Or has the poor chap one leg slightly shorter than the other? Davy James, for one, knows the score, having himself been a preparatory school pupil in a previous lifetime at dear old St Saviour's, over the hill but not so far away.

Inside the porch the vicar nails a small wreath, made from holly and ivy and studded with forbidden fruits, to the door of the church. As he steps back to survey his handiwork he hears a cough from behind him, then a chorus of youthful voices in droll unison.

Good afternoon, vicar.

Davy, Zibby, Murdo, Erica and Ted stand in a rough line before God's representative on earth, or His consul general in our minor outpost at least, with, clutched at arm's length in front of them, one shop window dummy apiece. Zibby's mannequin is dressed to look like Joseph, or in a way that conforms to stock notions of what Joseph looks like as seen in any of a thousand nativity plays and crib scenes the length and breadth of our county. Thus, we have the beard and the headdress with flaps hanging down, the dun tunic plus the rope for a belt. The facial expression, alas, is fixed – restricted, that is, by the technology available, to a visionary stare and an enigmatic smile. And perhaps that is exactly as it should be. So it is, too, for the other four mannequins, all of them suitably got up and gazing on life with equal missionary certitude in the hands of Zibby's classmates. Davy has his arms around the Virgin Mary, while Erica, Ted and Murdo sponsor a wise man each.

'Season's greetings, Joseph, and welcome, Mary,' says the vicar, spreading his arms, hammer in hand. Now he bows just a little for the benefit of the three wise men. 'Gentlemen – have you come far?'

'You could say, vicar,' Ted pipes up immediately.

'We followed a star,' Erica admits. 'In the east, I believe it was.'

'Took us ages, vicar,' Murdo confides. 'We had to eat our ass at one point.'

After Murdo has finished braying like a donkey the vicar shakes his head sadly at the ragtag assembly, and, of course, it appears his disappointment is directed principally at the choirboy, or the former choirboy, located somewhere in the middle of the group.

'One expects better, Davy. Just take them to the shed, please.'

As the classmates shuffle off with their biblical burdens towards a sizeable lean-to at the side of the church, their solemn journey is the occasion for an outbreak of themed singing.

'We three kings of Orient are,' Murdo begins in a surprisingly useful voice.

'Bearing gifts we –'

'Yes, thank you, Edward,' the vicar says.

'Thank you for what, vicar?' Ted calls out over his shoulder.

Covered overhead with corrugated iron but open on three sides to the elements, the spacious lean-to attached to the parish church on its west side is partly dressed already for the nativity scene, thanks in large measure to the gift from an anonymous donor of real straw in bales, and the two astonished sheep, these last stuffed locally five years ago with just such a setting in mind and leased to the village in perpetuity by old man Murphy. As a manger zone the environment has potential, although the crib-to-be, a lightweight basket of the sort often used for picking raspberries, remains unoccupied at this time. Of clothes suitable for the swaddling of infants there is no sign. What happens now begins well enough but then deviates sharply, rapidly and inevitably in the face of hormonal forces and the reliable instinct for cruelty of the adolescent mind. It kicks off with Davy's dancing. Although his classmates have discarded their mannequins already, Davy takes a different tack under the corrugated roof of the lean-to. Is he perhaps intent on bringing the roof down around him? Why would he move against himself so destructively? These linked ideas and arguments, barely touched on in his hard-working imagination but nonetheless present in the ether, the youth files in a box marked difficult to fathom. Actions, on the other hand, have consequences direct or indirect – this much he knows from experience. Might that be why he waltzes so freely and so recklessly around the lean-to now with his unlikely dance partner, the Virgin Mary?

'One expects better, Davy,' Zibby Saunders observes gravely from the wings. 'One expects much, much better.'

Is there something sexually or spiritually transgressive in the act of slow dancing with the mother of Jesus? Does the close presence of an audience make it better or worse, and what do the terms better and worse mean in this context? As Davy prepares to address these questions inside his head, he finds himself set upon by Murdo and Ted, one from in front and one from behind, with the result that he ends up in the dirt, mouth forced harshly against the cold lips of his dance partner. He is actually lying on top of Mary now with Murdo and Ted riding his body and calling him names, including bum-boy, which he has heard before, but not as an accompaniment to assault or battery or fisticuffs.

'Give it to her,' Ted exhorts, excited and a little breathless. 'Let her have it –'

'You know she wants it,' Murdo adds, twisting Davy's arm a bit higher up his back. 'You know you want it, Davy.'

For a few moments they speak ill of him, and although he hits out as hard as he can with his one free arm, he is obliged to concede that, for all practical purposes, his physical destiny is in the hands of his classmates. Zibby and Erica, fully engaged now with the whole puerile episode, are busy pulling hair and raining blows in a better-late-than-never attempt to end it. At all times the two sheep look on, astonished, from the sidelines. But is that snow that falls in a sly flurry from a squadron of brown clouds slinking southwards with territorial ambition from the general direction of Scotland?

'Enough!' cries the vicar from somewhere very close. Soon they are all standing again and looking pretty sorry for themselves. Soon they are on their feet, but the Virgin Mary is flat on her back in the dirt, a little of Davy's blood on her lips. As the shocked vicar gathers the dummy tenderly in, he rallies and relents. 'Bethlehem, boys,' he whispers, shaking his head all over again. 'Bethlehem, girls –'

33

It is definitely snowing now – a hard, dry matter which appears as if from nowhere a few feet above their heads and which stings the face and ears, especially the ears, with the effect of hail. As she makes her way alongside Davy from the lean-to towards the gate, Zibby pauses on the great flagstones in front of the church doors.

'Is it true?' she asks.

'What do you care?' Davy asks her in return.

'I don't,' she tells him, ducking inside the open porch.

'OK –' he says, joining her beside a vicar's wreath that hangs on the door. 'I'll tell you. But first you have to promise me something.'

'Don't worry,' Zibby says, adjusting her scarf in order to cover her mouth and chin. 'I won't blab, if that's what you're thinking.'

'That's not what I'm thinking. Will you promise to partner me in the Scramble?'

'What?'

'You heard me.'

'Bugger off, boyo. There's no way I'm squatting for half a bloody hour in some smelly old pram while all the people I dislike most in the world hurl abuse at me. Not for anyone. And especially not for you, darling.'

'So, you're chicken, are you?'

'You're having a laugh, aren't you, Davy James? Do I have to spell it out for you? All *right* – no girl's going to partner you in the stupid Scramble unless you *pay them*.' Having delivered this candid assessment Zibby exits the porch and backs away through the veil of snow towards the gate. Then she stops and ponders for a second or two. 'So, it's true, then?'

He is standing just inside the porch. When he dabs his lower lip with his cuff there is blood, but he doesn't think about it at this time. He stares her out until she shrugs at last and turns away. 'Zibby,' he calls. She stops again, and he goes on. 'Thanks,' he shouts. He means thanks for nothing – no, thanks for everything, everything that really matters in this wicked world. Thanks for this important endorsement and for that one. He knows what he means, but does she know?

'What for?' she calls out at the gate without even looking at him.

How foolish of him to consider her *for* him, or with him, or like him. She is just like all the others. When he can no longer view her receding form, Davy turns his back on the snow and faces the church door ever present with its sober wreath. He has had something more or less on his mind for half a bloody hour and now it confronts him with full force. It has to do with the stark wreath, which he uncouples there and then from its moorings in a swift act of larceny. He feels much stronger as a result. Antisocial though it is, this opportunistic intervention makes him strong, Davy decides with a bitter conviction born of humiliation and shame. There is a certain war memorial not far away that would benefit from such a wreath, the youth assures himself again in a last successful bid to scotch his qualms. Then he too quits the churchyard without looking back, leafy booty wrapped in his school blazer, and planting fierce footprints in the snow. The precipitation, rather heavy just a moment ago, drops off suddenly to leave the afternoon bright and clean.

CHAPTER SIX
This Version of Beauty

IN THE NEAR DARK SHE PRESSES A BRASS BELL set into the granite block beside the great doors – the doors of the bank. She breathes in deeply to steady herself and shakes the drops from her umbrella in preparation for entering, or for something – she doesn't know quite what. The afternoon, which flirted with sunshine, has given way to evening with a renewed call for sleety showers, and now, in a narrow strip above the hills to the west, the remnants of the day make their last stand, all purple and gold. She doesn't spot this meteorological outcome. She is not much interested in the darkling sky – not today. First, the light comes on above her head – a harsh white light. Then the door opens almost noiselessly to advertise the disciplined lustre, at once welcoming and forbidding, of the banking hall interior.

'You asked to see me,' Lydia says.

He is standing very close to her on the threshold of the bank. He is tall, fifty at most, powerful enough, his grey hair worn surprisingly long, with sleeves rolled up and braces running over his shoulders. 'Please –' he says, stepping to one side now like a butler or a footman. 'Won't you come in?'

Moments later they are in the manager's preserve at the rear of the building. On the far side of the room is a rosewood desk with, on this side and facing the window, two elegant but businesslike chairs for the use of customers or clients. In other respects, this generously proportioned workplace is more like a domestic study than an office, furnished comfortably as it is in leather and dressed with hangings and ornaments from around the world. The light comes courtesy of two tasteful and well-used standard lamps, their shades tilted slightly off axis in a way that suggests informality rather than indolence or an absence of regard. In the grate the coal fire has burned down to a benign crust that glows red hot beneath.

'Davy has been here to see me,' Saunders says carefully, pouring the second of two whiskies from a crystal decanter at a drinks station on one side of the room.

'What did you tell him?' Lydia asks, tugging at a glove with her teeth as she takes in first the Christmas cards on the mantlepiece and then the framed photograph, a black and white portrait of a woman, that sits on a bookcase below the good practice certificates and a pair of carved masks that must be from Africa. Although she has been in this room before, she finds it different today in its detail. Why is that?

'About the fund, you mean?' Saunders says. 'I told him nothing – as you stipulated from the beginning.'

'No one,' Lydia says, 'must know, as far as is possible, about the grant – least of all Davy himself. To be singled out like that because my means are insufficient to cover his school fees – it wouldn't be fair on him. And to *feel* set apart in such a way – Davy would find it intolerable. God knows the boy is already a target for gossip, or the butt of unkind jokes, on account of my circumstances.' Here Lydia stops to consider. Has she talked or said too much? It has all tumbled out rather, she tells herself, and with the look and feel of something many times rehearsed.

'Your son is a remarkable young man,' Saunders says, turning to face her finally with the two glasses in hand. When she shakes her head, he nods and sets the glasses down again. 'I believe he cares for you very much. Put another way, he worries about you – and it.'

'It?'

'Money, of course.'

'Whatever must you think of me, my dear Mr Saunders, when a mere schoolboy conducts my financial affairs behind my back?'

'I continue to think what I've thought for some time.'

'That the lady is a reckless spendthrift – an inveterate gambler, a socialite?' What does he think? Lydia discovers she doesn't actually know. What does he want? She needs to find out. If her irony is laid down as a challenge, it is one he takes up readily enough, parrying her shortness of tone without effort because, as the trappings of the room attest, he is nothing if not a man of the world.

'It is true,' he says, 'that you have certain outgoings or expenses. These are very much the expenses of a woman alone and of modest means, an educated woman who has raised a child on her own.'

'We have something in common,' Lydia notes with a wry laugh as, for a brief moment, she pictures Zibby Saunders, the daughter she barely knows but likes well enough. Why is she so defensive, then, in the presence of the girl's father? Surely it cannot be because she herself is poor while he clearly is not. Is it, perhaps, because he is so comfortable in his own skin? Or is it because she takes for granted, wrongly as it turns out, his disapproval of her as a mother?

'I don't,' he tells her, 'underestimate your achievement. A child successfully raised is, to my way of thinking, a long-term investment and an insurance policy.'

'Successfully raised?' she says, and she feels the temperature rise abruptly although she has long since taken off her gloves and coat.

'Children –' Saunders says, shrugging amiably. 'They are apt to end up paying for our mistakes, are they not?'

'Don't patronise me, sir, if that is what you set out to do.'

'Look —' he says with his wide-ranging patience. 'Let's face facts, shall we? You have your war widow's pension, and your job here in the village, of course. Meanwhile, your son's school shoes have holes in them and the roof of your house benefits likewise from unwelcome ventilation. Am I right so far?'

'You find this amusing?' she asks him.

'I find it affecting,' he tells her. 'I believe it affects me because you do.'

Ah, now she sees it. Fiduciary, financial, emotional, romantic – his stake in this conversation takes many shapes and forms. But can she count on the sincerity of his motive across these and other key categories? 'Davy will be leaving school soon enough,' she says, as if this might be a solution to something yet to show its hand.

'Davy is a young man,' Saunders says in the voice of experience. 'He has his own life to lead.'

'Davy is my son,' she says. 'I am perfectly aware of who he is and what he is.' She has been sitting opposite Saunders on one of two small settees, but now she gets up and moves to the side of the room, to the wall with its certificates and African masks. She has her back to the bank manager now with the bookcase and the black and white photograph in front of her. 'I'm sorry,' she says. 'Why did you ask me here today?'

'What are you hiding from, Lydia?' There – he has used her first name without her having sanctioned its use. What does it represent if not a turning point in their dealings with each other? 'What are you running from, I wonder?' he goes on. 'I want to help you – don't you see that?'

'Your wife was beautiful,' she says. When she turns away from the wall, he is standing very close to her. Gently, without looking at it, he prises the framed photograph from her hand, then returns it to its rightful place on the bookcase.

'Don't run from me, Lydia,' he says. 'Don't hide from me.'

'My son is a stranger,' she says with eyes cast down. 'I will never be young again. Do you imagine I still care what other people think of me?' Thus, in a few sentences, she sets out for anyone who chooses to listen the principles of her existence as she sees it. She is aware he has raised her chin up with his gentle finger. Did she feel it? She is not sure she is capable of feeling anything any more. 'I'm sorry,' she tells him again. 'I should go now.'

But he is not done with her – not yet. 'I ask only,' he says, 'that you promise to let me know when you need something. Anything. Do you suppose *I* still care what the world thinks of *me*? These things can always be arranged here – I mean in this room.'

'You're very kind,' she says, sweeping up her gloves.

'On the contrary,' Saunders says, helping her into her coat from behind. 'I find myself acting with a generous pinch of self-interest.' Then, when she turns to face him, he goes on. 'You asked me just now what I told Davy in respect of his bursary.'

'You said you told him nothing.'

'That's correct. But, in fact, he already suspects. How could he not?'

'He asked you straight out?'

'Yes – but, as I indicated earlier, I gave nothing away. And Davy understood very well my position here at the bank. That is why he is a scholarship boy with a bursary, is it not?'

'You should know that Davy is not quite – I mean not officially – a scholarship boy. The school funding, which is awarded here on an exceptional basis, is more of a hardship grant, as I understand it. But I am not too proud to accept a little charity on behalf of my son.'

He nods. He is nodding. Now there is only a handbag and a wet umbrella in the space between them. 'What takes place on Saturday in the James household?' he enquires in a brand-new voice, a much younger voice.

'This Saturday?' she says in the knowledge that an unusual thing is happening, or that something is changing, right here in this place. Now the room looks different to her. Now the room feels different to her. Lydia doesn't know how or why. She knows she doesn't trust herself to be happy – it is on this basis that she is accustomed to living life. 'I imagine,' she adds, lightheaded suddenly, 'I may take in a little washing or ironing to keep my creditors at bay. Since you ask –'

'Good,' he says. 'Then you're coming on a picnic.'

'A picnic?' she says, thrown further off guard by the agreeable novelty of the idea. 'May I remind you it's almost Christmas?'

'Exactly. It's a Christmas picnic.' Now he presents her with her loosely furled umbrella as if to confirm the arrangement. 'We'll pick you up at twelveish. Davy, too – I think Zibby's taken a shine to him, by the way. In my new car, I mean. Fearfully swish, I'm afraid. I do hope you enjoy car travel.'

'How lovely,' she says, smiling uncertainly, but smiling just the same. 'I believe Davy gets sick in motorcars.'

She has her raised umbrella in one hand, her handbag in the other. Inside the handbag, in addition to the usual items, are to be found Lydia's torch and a hastily assembled bunch of winter flowers gifted earlier this afternoon at the Post Office in an act of solidarity by her colleague, Betty, and comprising snapdragons, snowdrops, pansies and violas in gay profusion. The air must be a degree or so milder – now the sleet falls as rain on Lydia's torn umbrella as she makes her way in an ambulatory dream towards the so-called new cemetery, a

41

kind of overspill adjunct of the two older church graveyards, on the edge of the village where the lakeside road takes up.

She is quite alone. Out here on the perimeter the street lamps are fewer and further between. As she goes, Lydia tries not to think. She tries not to think about the scene that has just unfolded in the office of the bank manager. To think about it would be to begin to give it context and meaning – two things Lydia is anxious to avoid at this time unless they relate specifically to the mission now in train. What happened back there – it was a trick of the light, an illusion, having two complementary but conflicting facets. There was an offer on the part of the bank manager to look after her, or to look out for her. How touching and moving the unexpected kindness of others. Although she wouldn't actively seek help – not in a million years – the idea that someone might offer it means a lot to Lydia. Of course, he wants something in return. A man of the world is, after all, a man. There was the fact of the physical intimacy, too, wasn't there? Did it mark an unwarranted and unwelcome crossing of the line? Where should such a line be drawn? Lydia doesn't know. She lacks practice, quite simply – that is the whole trouble. And now there is the further prospect to contend with of a motorcar outing and a family picnic. Perhaps, Lydia tells herself distractedly, it will snow too heavily for picnics on Saturday. If anything, though, the air grows milder.

She shuts the wooden gate behind her. Ahead of her in the place where several paths converge she can clearly see the memorial to the village fallen – in a melodramatic gesture the silvery obelisk rises up to slash, as and when the chance presents, the slim December moon. Already Lydia can see something – a shape, an outline – at the lower edge of her vision. She takes out her torch and, moving downwards from the top, scans the names carved in capital letters into the stone of the plinth. These thirteen names she knows off by heart. In the

42

case of a few – WILLIAM ARTHUR BLAIR or THOMAS JOHN INNES, for example – she can even put a face to the name. About half way down the list is the name that means most to her. The name SCOTT EDWARD JAMES is mid-way down a register arranged in alphabetical order by surname. For a moment or two Lydia attends to the stone of the memorial in this exact zone with the beam of her torch, using a tender back and forth motion that amounts to a caress. There is no other way to describe how it feels to her and how it might look to anyone watching. After a short time, she scans downwards as far as the base of the plinth. It is as she thought – some do-gooder has left a wreath made from holly and ivy and studded with shiny berries at the foot of the monument. Although the wreath is small in scale it is particularly fine, and this fineness it is which overwhelms Lydia and causes her to change her mind suddenly about her battered posy of winter blooms. Such flowers, she decides, would look better at home in a vase at the kitchen window. She is disappointed and saddened – of course she is. But there is something else, is there not? The nice judgement she arrives at after weighing this version of beauty against that one is a marvellous construct, an ideal thing. Viewed in the right light it represents a type of new beginning or a fresh start for Lydia, which is why she allows herself a tiny sliver, scant as the new moon, of exultation as she embraces the darkness at the edge of the village. Oh, look – the Christmas lights are showing outside Müller's hotel.

PART SECOND
Death by Dreaming

FROM THE BEGINNING I HAD TAUGHT Latin at St Saviour's, a boys-only preparatory school for both boarders and day pupils tucked as far away as possible from the prying eye of the modern world in one of the timeless valleys that are ten a penny in these parts. I recall a privileged landscape of sloping rugby fields and waterlogged cricket squares that was also a disciplined learning environment in which the character-building benefits of corporal punishment and the cold shower were taken for granted by staff and pupils alike. I remember – I will always remember – the casual cruelty of pubescent boys in relation to my disability, or my deformity as they termed it. And, of course, I remember the young Davy James.

'Why is your left leg shorter than your right leg, Mr Darling?' he asked me urgently at the lunch table one day in Michaelmas term, not because he didn't know the answer – they all did – but because he wanted to hear me say it in my own words and in my own way.

Exactly why Davy was withdrawn from St Saviour's is unclear to me. What was the matter with him? As far as I knew he had done nothing to warrant his expulsion or rustication – he hadn't, to my knowledge, been discovered smoking cigarettes behind the cricket pavilion or slumbering fitfully in a boarder's bed at midnight. Was there something wrong with Davy? Had he some eating disorder yet to be disclosed, or a debilitating illness as yet undiagnosed? Was he seeking attention? Or was he simply crying out, as so many of our young men do, for help in the face of an unanswerable expectation? We don't know. We know his mother was viewed locally as a discreet alcoholic, and the funds available to her for private schooling would have been limited, to say the least.

It was Lydia who asked me to tutor her son in Latin two evenings each week at the cold stone house on the northern shore of the lake. When she set her payment terms somewhat below what was usual, I accepted them anyway, not because I have no need of money but rather because I have neither interest in, nor taste for, the material world. And Lydia was a sometime tutor to Davy too – the mother drew for educational guidance and inspiration as best she could on an old edition of Encyclopædia Britannica that lay around the house, a volume here, a volume there. No one knew where this formidable resource had come from – nevertheless, it was an accepted part of the James household along with the creaking stairs and the draught from the bay window that looked onto the lake. For the mother these pedantic volumes full of facts had a quality that was almost sacred or divine. To my mind this respect for knowledge and understanding was an expression by proxy of her love for a son who would need to know *everything* if he was to make his way in life. If Lydia had a feeling for the deep needs of others it was because she shared, in a way that was largely unspoken, their innermost pain. For example, she never once asked me about my limp or my special shoe.

Then one day in early spring Davy enrolled at his new school in the village. There was talk at that time of a bursary or a grant. The idea was put about that he was a scholarship boy, although no one seemed to know for certain, least of all the youth himself. His mother had her job behind the counter at the village Post Office, plus her widow's pension, of course, but it was understood widely within our interested community that these would scarcely have yielded funds enough for her needs.

So, it ended – my tenure as a private tutor to the son of the James household. When I think of this period, I see Davy sitting opposite me at the kitchen table, Kennedy's Revised Latin Primer open face down in front of him, and reciting for my sake only some mnemonic or aide-memoire I had drilled him in two or three days earlier. *He throws a fit of righteous wrath at -bo, -bis, -bit in third and fourth.* In fact, the business of the Latin defined this time for all of us. The mother, who knew nothing of Latin in practice, had, even so, an instinctive regard for its power and influence. As for Davy – when I asked him why he wanted to learn the dead language he shrugged and said *because it's a hard thing to do, isn't it?* It's true I had grown rather fond of him. It was obvious to me even then he was intent on punishing himself for being different – for being, in other words, just as he was. I recognised that damaging instinct right away because I have followed its path myself since I was Davy's age or younger. If only he could have seen it – his identity was his destiny, nothing more and nothing less.

At around this time, it should be noted for the record, I began to dream about Davy James. These dreams quickly became so vivid that I felt compelled, as a would-be storyteller, to jot them down as soon as I woke up. Mostly the dreams were associated with Davy in an oblique or tangential way. That is to say he was part of the dream only to the extent that he was witnessing what was taking place. He was, in other words, a substitute for me. The funny thing about these dreams was the recurring motif within them of the deer. In the first such scenario Davy watches from the kitchen window as a juvenile doe, chased to the edge of the lake by a slavering wolf, plunges into the water, only to discover on kicking out that the lake has become, without prior notice or consultation, the open sea at a time of storm. There was no need to mine these subconscious narratives for hidden meaning – their sub-text of hazard or jeopardy was all too visible at the surface. Yet as one dream gave way to another in my breakfast notebook, their visual tone and tenor increasingly strident or shrill, I began to suspect I was laying the foundation for the story, complete and unabridged, of my own brilliant death by self-regard.

CHAPTER EIGHT
A New World Record

IT IS COLD – THIRTY-FOUR DEGREES FAHRENHEIT according to a thermometer nailed to the wall of the log cabin in a small clearing high on a forested hill. Adam Boyd is up early. He is out and about on his beloved hillside, his rifle in his hands. It doesn't matter what make of rifle it is. The calibre and bore – they hardly matter either. The rifle is ideally suited to slaying wild animals or birds – fauna of all stripes. That is the only thing that matters. As a single shot firearm this rifle is supremely accurate. It has to be – there will be no second chance for the hunter confronted by a mortally wounded lioness in Tanganyika, for example, and, by the same token, there is no second barrel with which to administer the coup de grâce. Such a rifle must be in the right hands, of course, and Adam's are nothing if not right. That is why he is employed to shoot game by old man Murphy, who owns half of our county, and who takes very seriously the business of managing the land on behalf of future generations of the Murphy family. Adam, in common with his landed boss, is no sentimentalist. Hunting and shooting – these are among the things he does best.

It is cold. It is early, much too early for the feeble sun to arrive, huffing and puffing and dragging its heels as usual up some slope or other until it crests and then clears, with a cry of *just look at me now*, the craggy ridges in the east. At this time of year, the morning mist sits in the valley, like used bathwater in the tub, to a level roughly half way up the incline of the hill, to a level just below the tree line. Today, Adam Boyd takes up position a few yards above one notional line and a few yards below another. But although he locates himself at this height on the hillside, in the zone between mist and tree line, he is not stationary at these latitudes. Rather he makes his way across the tangled surface of the hill at a constant height above sea level as if to describe his own Tropic of Cancer. It is here, in a region where warmer currents clash with colder and the trees give way to moor and sky, that the exhilarated birds and beasts of the hill are at their most willing to take a bullet.

There is a red deer up ahead, an ancient buck with grey winter coat and branched antlers almost too heavy to bear after fifteen years on this happy hillside. The red deer is alone once again, the rutting season being over – now he forages hard for some tender morsels among the dwarf plants and immature trees on the border between woodland and moor. And although he cannot actually smell Adam Boyd, who is at least fifty yards downwind of him, the deer is aware of the gamekeeper's distant presence in a way he is unable to explain. Is there a holy bond, an unwritten memorandum of understanding, between hunter and hunted such as exists between blood brothers? Adam likes to think so. After all, he has had his eye on this old boy for three weeks now, and the cull is not yet ended. And the deer feels something similar in his turn. After three weeks of daily intimacy the beast has come to love the man who would down him with a single shot. As Adam loads his rifle with the buckshot cartridge his thoughts turn very naturally to what the highly experienced but still sensitive red deer might be thinking at this precise moment. As for the deer – he is thinking something like *please don't shoot me today for I have not yet done what I was put here to do.* And Adam senses this because he is in

52

tune, as people are wont to remark, with nature. He is like the first man who ever walked these hills. He is like the first man ever to roam these valleys. That is why his name is Adam. Now a shot rings out, but the deer is not downed today.

At that very instant – the instant of Adam Boyd's report – Lydia wakes up with a start in the old stone house beside the lake and below the hill. It is still dark in this shuttered room. Lydia jumps up in bed. It's as if a rifle, a rifle or a shotgun, has just gone off inside her head – try as she might, Lydia is unable to remember the dream, if dream it was. Immediately her thoughts turn to the man who has the gun. Who else but Adam Boyd fits the bill here? That is what Lydia asks herself as she scrabbles around for the alarm clock on the nightstand beside the half-empty bottle and a glass. And this could be any time of year. This could be any day of the week, with or without school, with or without work. We are all connected to these hills and these valleys, Lydia thinks in a moment of extreme loneliness. We are all connected to each other, she thinks sadly. For some reason she calls out Davy's name. Then she sinks back down with a little groan and listens out for it. She is waiting for the drop to land in the bucket in the corner of the room, but there is no drop today.

A whistle blasts shrilly – this intrusive accessory on a lanyard belongs to Mr Lees, sadistic PE instructor and cheating husband of Mrs Lees, the kindly but meddlesome choir mistress who collects funds for the Scramble in her public-spirited pram.

Davy James, pale limbs extending shyly from shorts and singlet, runs the length of the school gymnasium as, beside and behind him, his classmates queue up to take their next turn in a kind of physical loop or human round robin. As he runs, Davy's bare feet pound the floorboards. To left are the wall bars, to right the old ropes hanging

53

from the rafters to within a few feet of the floor. Up ahead, Davy can see the vaulting horse with, just beyond it, the muscular frame of Mr Lees, and, on this side and that, the outstretched arms of Murdo and Ted. These four arms are waiting to help Davy somersault over the horse so that he lands, feet planted together and hands held out for balance, on a rubber carpet in front of the PE instructor. There is a problem, though, of timing – a problem exacerbated by the natural disinclination of Davy's two helpers to assist him. As he approaches the vaulting horse Davy can see what Mr Lees is unable to see – a delegation of school governors, led by Miss Montgomery and intent on observing the head teacher's progressive mixed class ideas at first hand, has just this second appeared in the corner of the gymnasium nearest the door. Thus distracted at the climax of his run-up, Davy bundles himself awkwardly and in several half-hearted stages from one side of the horse to the other before regrouping gamely on the mat at the rear of the apparatus. He knows the score – they all do. Girls jump, or vault, the horse. Boys do otherwise.

'Somersaults, Davy,' hisses Mr Lees after spitting his whistle out disdainfully. 'What is it that boys do when they get their chance at the vaulting horse?'

'Somersaults, sir,' Davy confirms cheerfully, with nary a trace of bitterness or rancour, because it is really no one's fault, and life is so often arbitrarily unjust. 'Boys *somersault –*'

'Are you a man or a mouse?' Lees asks, following up needlessly and dismissively with a shake of the head.

From Murdo's throat issues an opportunistic squeak, which the PE instructor appears to sanction or condone – certainly he takes no steps to question or condemn it. That is OK with Davy. It is water off a duck's back to Davy James. Watch him now as he lines up once more at the back of the queue. He smiles relentlessly on life as the whistle sounds again and, at the edge of his vision, Zibby Saunders goes on to clear the horse effortlessly and unaided.

'Well?' Davy says, addressing both Erica and Janice who are in front of him and deep in conversation towards the back of the queue. He has given these two female classmates several minutes to consider his proposition, and by now they will have come to a decision. It just needs one of them to acquiesce, Davy tells himself. It only needs one of them to seal the deal.

'Don't take this the wrong way,' says Janice, an entirely sensible young woman whose mother, the soul of village discretion, runs the handy grocery shop and off-sales where Lydia James buys much of her gin. 'It's nice to be asked and all that. It's just that –'

'It's just that –' Erica takes up helpfully on behalf of her friend before being interrupted. The whistle has gone again. When will it leave off? As she shoves Janice forward to take another turn at the horse, pushy Erica tells Davy exactly what she thinks of his generous offer. 'It's just that no one in their right mind is going to partner *you*, Davy. Now, fuck off and die, choirboy.'

That is such a harsh verdict on everything. There is no call for such a nasty rejoinder. He is running towards the horse. Now there is only the horse and Davy – there is nothing and no one else in this cold cathedral, a shrine to enmity and adverse feeling. This horse is his friend, Davy tells himself. No right-thinking horse would forsake him. There is a sloping board immediately in front of the horse – a kind of launch pad or platform. Davy takes off here as never before and, disdaining hasty offers of assistance from his classmates on both sides, turns in the air one and a half times before crashing to the floor at the edge of the mat. The schoolboy can no longer see the school's governors. For a few moments he can't see anything at all unless it happens to be located already on the inside of his head.

He is running and running in his shorts and vest. He is barefoot in the streets of the village, turning heads, causing cars and bicycles and the butcher's van to swerve alarmingly. Look – there goes Mrs Lees with her pram of plenty. There stands Betty, brave and loyal friend of Davy's mother – see how she watches him streak past the window of the Post Office. And there is Mr Saunders. The bank manager is there too, waving what looks to be a five pound note like a punter at the gee-gees. Oh, here comes Miss Montgomery marshalling a posse of school governors. They are all present and correct. They are all in on the act, whatever the act might be. It matters not to Davy. He knows exactly what he is doing. He knows exactly where he is going. His overarching mission or ambition is to see a man about a dog.

When he reaches Adam Boyd's caravan in the grounds of the Abercrombie Hotel he bangs on the door with the flat of his hand. No response. Hold on a minute – is it Rachel or Victoria or someone completely different who blows perfectly formed smoke rings at him from behind the net curtain? Not to worry and never to mind. He is on his way again. He is on a hillside. He is on a wooded hillside, legs aching, feet bleeding. Up ahead is a shack, a log cabin of the type used by gamekeepers in films. The door of the cabin stands ajar – it is like an open invitation to Davy, out of puff as he is and observed by phantom rabbits. It is just as he imagined it would be. The whole thing is turning out just the way he expected. This gamekeeper's hut is rough and ready. There is the rough wooden table and the rough wooden chair and the iron bed pushed up against the dirty window. And a rusting paraffin stove. On the table is a selection of dead game – a rabbit, a hare, a brace of red grouse. Although no one is present in the gamekeeper's hut the stove is lit – Davy can see the warm glow at its belly, and this is the sign he has been looking for all his life.

One crocodile, two crocodile, three crocodile –

As he backs out of the gamekeeper's hut Davy begins the count inside his head. Cut to a hillside stream that flows quick and clear around the rocks and the grassy tufts. It looks like Davy is actually in the stream. Yes, he is. He is flat on his back in the icy current, elbows tucked in and eyes closed tightly. And still he counts out the seconds as accurately and as fairly as he possibly can, giving due attention to each one before discarding it in favour of the next, his cracked voice reaching up now to the tops of the trees and the sky.

Sixty-six crocodile, sixty-seven crocodile –

Davy is still counting when Adam raises him up. The schoolboy stands like a wobbly statue dripping onto the floor of the forest. The gamekeeper has his tweed jacket off – now he drapes it around the schoolboy's shoulders, which are shaking, and buttons it at the front.

'I wanted to tell you something,' Davy says, but in fact the words won't come out, or they come out wrong because the youth's teeth are chattering, or doing what teeth do under these atmospheric or emotional conditions. What was it he wanted to tell Adam Boyd? It must have been something very important to come all this way, feet bleeding and without a scarf. Was it something special and true?

'You're all right now, Davy,' Adam says, gathering the boy in.

'Sixty-seven seconds, Adam – a new world record, must be.'

'A new world record it is, son. Now, let's get you home.'

He is conscious, awake. He has the sensation of being wet, and there is a rushing sound in his ears. He is lying flat on his back on the floor of the gym with all the faces looking down on him at close quarters. There is nothing wrong with him. He feels no real pain. Even so, he thinks – this is what it must be like to be dead or dying. You are on the ground. You are lying flat on your back with a circle of shocked faces peering down at you. They are rooting for you, the concerned citizens to whom these anxious faces belong. Why else are they here? Then you hear the siren – it gets louder as it draws nearer. Now it grows fainter. It recedes a bit. That is because it is no longer intended for you. Perhaps it never was.

As he lies star-shaped, centre of excitable attention now, on the gymnasium floor, these and other unhelpful influences assail Davy, undermining his self-esteem and damaging his chances of finding a partner for the Scramble. Are those Zibby's features bearing down on him from the ring of leering faces? No doubt she harbours hopes that a certain impending picnic will have to be cancelled now, or at least postponed until the cows come home. But Davy is OK. True, he has felt better. But he is OK. And although he would happily skip the famous picnic himself, when push comes to shove he has already made up his mind. The event, which is tied up in some mysterious way with the future, or with the whole idea of personal destiny, will go ahead as planned. Some episodes are like forks in the road, aren't they? The meaning of these gateway happenings goes beyond their face value. They must be recognised for what they are and embraced – for good or ill, for better or worse. At least the narcissistic whistle has stopped its shrieking, Davy notes gratefully, bringing his eyelids down hard in a bid to blot out the picture of his life. Even the sound of water in his head is fading now. Credit where credit is due.

CHAPTER NINE
Love Me Tender

SATURDAY DAWNS, BRIGHT AND BEAUTIFUL. It's a lovely day in a lovely part of the world. With a gloved hand on the steering wheel of his brand-new Daimler Regency saloon, Saunders waits patiently for a knot of bovine backsides, currently blocking the car's progress through the village, to disperse as, beside him in the passenger seat, her eyes glued to the arse of a cow, his principal guest focuses hard on ignoring the untimely attentions of passers-by. Lydia has dressed sensibly for what is, after all, an outdoor occasion, eschewing make-up in the prevailing spirit of pragmatic engagement. She looks good because she is a good-looking woman. In the back of the vehicle are Davy and Zibby, the one intent on replacing an ashtray in the door beside him, the other leaning out of the window with what looks like an 8mm cine camera at her eye. Unlike the woman who sits in front, the bank manager's daughter cuts a dash, with sunglasses perched fashionably atop a polka-dot headscarf she wears knotted at the chin. Her cherry red lipstick is precocious. As for the two males within the group – they look much as they always do on Saturday morning.

'Better back off a bit, Dad,' ventures Zibby, leaning forward to check on the cows.

'John Wayne and Co –' Saunders remarks, then honks his horn. 'Never around when you actually need them.' When he glances at

Lydia, she rewards him with a smile. We are in this together, she is thinking. We are all of us connected to these lovely hills and valleys.

'Got to be old man Murphy,' Davy offers in the voice of mature reason, glad beyond words suddenly that he has chosen to remove the ridiculous bandage from his head.

And, indeed, Murphy is there, right on cue, surrounded by his noisy and disoriented cows. After he works his way, slapping rumps, to the back of the herd, emerging finally a few yards in front of the stationary Daimler, he doffs his cap and bows low, ironically, for the benefit of the bank manager's party.

'Top of the morning, Murphy,' Saunders calls out, winding his window down further.

'More like afternoon in my book, Saunders,' Murphy fires back humorously, casting a sharp eye over the interior of the car. 'Lovely day for it, Mrs James,' he says with just the hint of a leer in his voice now, and without clarifying what *it* might refer to. 'Well – mustn't keep you good people. Streets is for cars, not cattle, these days – ain't that right, Davy?'

'If you say so, Mr Murphy –'

Here, the old boy runs a finger admiringly over the paintwork of the vehicle. 'Lovely job, Saunders –' he says, winking finally. 'I could do with some of that myself.'

'So, come and talk to us – that's what we're here for.' Now the cows have parted and the window is raised up on the driver's side. 'Don't hide it all under the mattress,' Saunders concludes *sotto voce* with a cheery wave for Murphy and a smile in the direction of Lydia.

'That awful man –' she says, laughing. 'He always has a glint of something in his eye.'

'It's called brass,' Davy says, fretting with immediate effect over this oh-so-obvious stab at light comedy in case it should be viewed inside the car as resentful or covetous. And yet money, or the subject of money, can scarcely be forgotten or ignored here, given who these people are. Money is like the fifth occupant of this top-of-the-range motorcar. 'Soon he'll be drowning in cash,' Davy takes up, warming to his theme now. He doesn't care any more about saying the right thing or the wrong thing. He is talking about old man Murphy and his sale of prime land to a consortium of developers from Sheffield. 'Behold my enormous stash,' Davy declaims, regretting in a flash this choice of words. He has the camera trained on Zibby – she plays up to it, toying with her sunglasses and running her tongue over luscious lips. 'Crickey – not your material assets, I hope,' she says witheringly as they round the corner that separates village from countryside.

'Good luck to Murphy, I say,' Saunders says equably, resetting their conversational compass at a stroke. And, in fact, it is difficult to look unkindly on life at a time like this – the sky is impeccably blue, and the road, which runs straight as an arrow along the floor of the valley, is flanked on either side by raging streams and by evergreen armies descending to drink in victorious ranks. 'One day the canny old trout is slumming it in a rundown pile with dodgy plumbing, the next he's digging a swimming pool on the lawn.'

'I don't think it's a very popular move,' Lydia puts in because she probably ought, by now, to have expressed an opinion on this issue of Murphy and his sale. Progress, change – she doesn't distrust them as such. She just wonders what they might lead to.

'It's his land,' Saunders points out with a type of verbal shrug. 'Why should he worry about what people think? He's laughing all the way to the bank. To my particular bank, I trust –'

'I just hope they build houses,' Lydia says. 'Forget the hill and the childish Scramble that goes with it. What's to keep young people here when there's no decent houses to live in?'

'Who wants to live here anyway?' Zibby says before snatching her camera away from Davy. 'There's no film in it yet, stupid,' she tells him, disowning this last epithet for all kinds of reasons, some of which have to do with the presence, not far away, of Davy's mother. 'I'm getting just a trifle concerned, that's all,' she continues, fighting a rearguard action in terms of her tone. 'Do you think that fall in the gym might have knocked a few screws loose?'

'Are you an apologist for our infamous Scramble, Zibby?' asks Lydia, lending a slight edge to her enquiry, it seems, and targeting it more actively by half turning in her seat. 'Davy appears to be taking an extraordinary interest in it this year.'

'I suspect,' Saunders interposes, 'Zibby would rather record the whole circus for posterity.'

'I can't see what all the fuss is about, Mrs James.'

'Nor me, dear. I take it you won't be lining up at the start with Davy, then —'

If there is the suggestion here of an awkward silence, Saunders fills it rapidly using the tiniest suggestion of his good breeding. 'Have you picked out a partner yet, young man?'

'No, Mr Saunders.' Although at the front of the car the general feeling is one of warmth – consider the underlying sympathy of lone parents making common cause – the same can hardly be said of the back-seat atmosphere, reminiscent as this is of the Arctic Circle out of season. 'Not yet, I mean.'

'Negotiations are ongoing —' Saunders summarises tactfully.

'That's right, sir.' And, really, Davy feels quite nauseous at this point in time. Is it the car travel, which always does for him after half an hour or so? Or is it the lingering effect of his extensively publicised tumble in the school gymnasium? Either way, he must rally. Are you a man or a mouse, Davy James? 'As a matter of fact, negotiations are entering a highly critical phase,' he manages to say now. 'But do you think we could stop the car soon, please?'

The picnic spot turns out to be a swathe of grass on a shallow incline running down from a lay-by towards a swollen stream that flows fast and hard against the familiar backdrop of evergreen trees – pine, fir or spruce varieties that cloak the hillside to left and right as far as the eye can see. A tarpaulin will be necessary, for the ground is damp.

As Saunders and Zibby spread the tartan rug at the base of a solitary rowan, they can just about hear, above the rushing of the stream, the sound of Davy vomiting at a location not very far away to which he has taken himself off directly, his mother in attendance. Now father and daughter busy themselves with the not unpleasant task of ferrying comestibles and picnic stuffs in wicker hampers from the car to their chosen spot beneath the tree.

'That old Saunders charm seems to be working its magic,' the bank manager says as Davy retches for the final time. As she watches Lydia and Davy march slowly back up the slope, the brook flashing behind them, Zibby awaits her father's verdict on her conduct thus far – a verdict she knows must come, just as winter, or Christmas, must come. 'We have guests today,' he tells her. 'Do you imagine it's somehow clever or funny to make a guest feel awkward or foolish in our company? I assure you it's neither smart nor funny, Zibby. It's rather childish, as a matter of fact.'

She is thinking something along the lines of *I don't want to be here, Dad – you do.* In the event she takes a different tack. 'I'm sorry,' she says. 'He is a schoolboy until recently puking up, while she is some kind of shadow or ghost as far as I can tell.'

'Mrs James has just lost her job,' Saunders informs her. 'Let's try to bear that in mind, shall we?' Now that their little chat is over, he kneels on the rug and begins to set up a portable gramophone. Then he calls out to Lydia. 'Will Frank Sinatra do?'

'Frank Sinatra will do perfectly.'

'Just as well,' he shoots back affably, 'because Frankie-boy is all we have.'

'How's Davy?' Zibby asks, slipping a cartridge into her camera.

'Oh, he's all right,' Lydia says, spinning round full circle to take in the whole picturesque scene and the son that lags behind. 'I'm not sure I can speak for his appetite, though.'

'Extremely considerate of him,' Saunders says, 'to wait till he got out of a certain motorcar.' Then, as Davy nears their little group, he reiterates this point of view for the benefit of the youth. 'Sit yourself down, Davy. How do you feel? Better out than in, and all that –'

Davy says nothing. It's true he feels much better, this improving position associated with a comparatively low base. As he continues to stand just shy of the tartan rug he surveys the victuals spread out temptingly beneath the bare tree, taking in cold roasted game and fowl either pale or dark in jointed portions, sliced ham studded with what can only be cloves, a half loaf plus the butter in a dish, two or three cheeses hard or blue, and various expensive looking pâtés of what might be liver or pork set in ramekins or else got up in pastry. Of liquid refreshment there is as yet no sign. And to Davy marooned on the outskirts of life it seems this whole social construct is for other people, not him. Then it comes back to him with renewed force and weight – what he is doing here today. He is a young man with two jobs to do, and both of these jobs involve taking himself off without further delay. His mother – she must be left alone with the nice bank manager, surely, for a decent period at least. (The financial logic of this thinking seems blindingly obvious to the youth.) And to be alone with the bank manager's daughter will play into Davy's hands, or so he calculates. How else can he expect to make progress towards his key objective? 'Would you excuse me, please,' he says now, grabbing a half partridge and bolting towards the stream and the trees.

'Cue music,' Saunders says, addressing Zibby for the most part.

'Frank Sinatra gets stuck on one side,' she reminds him, picking up her camera and then running down the slope after Davy.

Now they are alone together, the widower and the widow. 'I'm so pleased you could come today,' Saunders tells Lydia. 'No – we're extremely pleased you could come.'

'I'm not convinced I'm very good company,' she says. Then, as if to echo or mirror his remarks, she adds her qualification. 'I'm not sure *we're* very good company today.' She smiles bravely enough at something – the trees, maybe – although it is really quite cold under the brittle blue sky. 'Did we pack hot soup?' she asks in friendly jest, rubbing her arms.

'If we didn't, we almost certainly should have,' he says, laughing and getting up easily from the picnic rug. 'Let me just check with the concierge,' he adds, loping towards the car that awaits his bidding at the crest of the rise.

As she gazes towards the stream she can hear the clink, getting closer now, of the glasses and the bottle – the bottle of what can only be, to her way of thinking, a fine champagne. 'It seems the mountain ash is less and less widespread,' she announces unaccountably.

'Look at me, Lydia,' he says. 'This is the way it begins.'

They are sitting facing one another astride a fallen tree. He has his partridge drumstick, and she has her cine camera. He is minded to bring up the subject of the Scramble as early as possible, but, in the event, the chance, if it can be so described, slips away from him. The main thing is this – he can't decide whether she is for him or against him, and this is obviously a crucial determinant in advance of any serious negotiations. When he goes back over the relevant ground he sees or hears only confusing signals and mixed messages coming from Zibby. What does that signify? Is it a mark of disrespect to play thus with someone's feelings? Or does it simply mean she is unsure of herself? She doesn't strike him as someone who is unsure of where she stands in relation to questions great and small. For her part, she thought she liked him well enough. No, she thought she liked him a lot. Then she wasn't so sure. In trying to uncover the nature of, and reason for, her equivocation she tip-toes her way towards a certain word. That word, which is *victim*, won't present itself to her at this stage. Still, she knows what she means. Yet there is something about him – a physical courage, she decides – that is striking and attractive. He is not afraid of a scrap. He is not afraid of a bare-knuckle fight – a dogfight with his own body (or soul, she might have added) if needs be, if it comes right down to it. This is how she views it. This is how she sees him. But, one way or another, he is no further forward in respect of his quest to win the Scramble.

She raises the camera to her eye and asks him to sing something. 'Anything you like,' she tells him. 'Or read me out a poem,' she says. 'Willows whiten, aspens quiver –'

'Little breezes dusk and shiver,' he says, finishing a couplet from English class before prising the camera from her fingers and turning it back on her. 'Is it loaded now?' he asks her, licking clean his own fingers as a kind of afterthought.

'You have to pull the trigger,' she tells him, 'as if you're firing a revolver in a dream.'

'Sing me something,' he says. 'Sing me anything you like.'

She gives him Love Me Tender, the first two verses only. *For, my darling, I love you and I always will.* He is unfamiliar with this song. Even so, he is moved by the lyric. Why has she chosen this particular song out of all the songs in the universe? Is she making fun of him? He doesn't know, once again, how to read her. She has stopped singing. She has observed for the first time the gash in his shoe. How old is that rent between sole and upper? How can she have missed it until now? As she takes it back from Davy, her cine camera strikes her as an unpardonable indulgence, a projection of her ego or vanity.

'You should be in the choir,' he tells her.

'I don't think Elvis would be quite right in that context,' she says.

'It's true the choir is really a state of mind,' he says.

'Don't you wish you were in America?' she says.

'I hadn't really thought about it,' he says.

'What goes on inside that pretty little head?' she says.

'Less than you might think,' he says after a short delay.

'Shouldn't you try to kiss me at this point?' she says.

'Probably,' he says.

'Are you going to?' she asks.

'What do you think?' he says as the car horn sounds three times from the lay-by above them. 'You can tell me later,' he adds, tossing a partridge bone over his shoulder and making fast for the stream and the road that, together, run forever west towards the sea.

They are sitting side by side in the car now, having reached a state of impasse. If she winds down her window and looks out, Lydia will just about be able to see the border of the tarpaulin and the glass of champagne – the one she has left untouched – that teeters on the grass below her. If she winds down her window a fraction, she will hear Sinatra sing to an abandoned feast.

'You think I'm just going through the motions,' she says, as if to pick up on his most recent comments. 'So what? Perhaps that's what

I'm best at. Perhaps that's the only way I know. One foot in front of the other – day in, day out.'

'We all have our graveyards to attend or attend to,' Saunders says. 'Our empty rooms –'

'Which the sun fails to penetrate?' she says. 'You think you know me I suppose. You think I need to throw wide the shutters and raise high the blinds.'

'I know myself,' he says. 'I know what I feel for you. What I need to know better is the depth of your feeling for Adam Boyd.'

'You forget yourself, sir,' she says, leaning across and stabbing at the car horn, but without audible result.

'Far from it,' he says. 'It's only now I begin to remember.' Here, he opens the door on his side and discards the contents of his goblet before sounding the car horn calmly three times. 'I'm sorry,' he goes on. 'No doubt you see yourself as something entire, fully made, out of reach or beyond rescue. But I have to think of you as something, or someone, other – someone dear, someone beautiful. And, yes – someone fallible.'

'Is this to be a seduction?' she says. 'You go too far.' As she sits beside him in the long silence various almost forgotten images catch up with her so that soon the veins stand out at her wrists above fists tightly clenched. The past, which she has worked so assiduously to leave behind her, is actively present in this car like an unscheduled passenger – a hitchhiker on the highway to tomorrow. For a moment she feels dirty, sinful, and although she understands very well it is not his fault, she moves quickly to blame the bank manager for allowing this to happen. What did he mean by it – *beyond rescue*. Did he mean beyond redemption? What did he intend by *fallible*? What does he really know? Then, just as quickly, she comes to her senses. The man beside her can know nothing. How could he? And what of it if he did? Meanwhile, the picnic items must be gathered in, and there is a journey to be made in the company of the daughter and the son. Suddenly Davy is here, hands on knees, panting a little from a recent exertion by the look of it, and moving to knock on the car window. Lydia winds the window down before the youth manages to make contact with the glass. And, in fact, she has never loved or resented him as much as she does during these interminable seconds. 'Time to pack everything up, darling,' she says. 'Mr Saunders agrees – it's really too cold for a picnic today after all.'

CHAPTER TEN

The Fourth Wise Man

INSIDE THE CHILLY CHURCH SOME FIFTEEN school-age children occupy the forward pews below the organ pipes and beside the large, illuminated Christmas tree. Clutching black hymn books, they chat among themselves with a mixture of seasonally adjusted excitement and instinctual respect for this spartan seat of worship. Davy is with them and at the same time separate from them – he sits on his own, chewing gum covertly several rows back from the lateral choir stalls in the main body of the church and daring himself to blow a bubble (an impulse he resists because a stronger, stranger idea is even now casting off from a little used jetty in his brain). Quite simply he won't risk joining these other members of the choir in case they reject him either verbally or physically. That it has come to this inside his pretty little head is the cause of much pain to the youth. His alienation from his peers he experiences clearly enough, although he wouldn't know how to articulate or describe the whole sorry business – not without recourse to this or that entry in Encyclopædia Britannica. Together or apart these youthful singers await the arrival inside the church of the choir mistress, who is unusually and unaccountably late tonight, for what may well be their last practice session this side of Christmas. Now the double doors behind Davy open with an unholy clatter to admit, breathless and for a second time, the vicar himself.

70

'As you were, ladies and gentlemen, boys and girls – Mrs Lees has telephoned to say her bicycle has miraculously reappeared in the cupboard under the stairs where she presumably neglected to look for it in the first place.' As he backs away and begins to draw the big doors closed again the vicar cannot resist adding, at pulpit volume, his partisan postscript. 'God moves, as I'm sure we all recognise by now, in mysterious ways his wonders to perform.'

Once the doors have closed the chatter takes up again with new vim. Davy is on his feet. He is in the aisle. He turns his back on the altar and makes his way from the church unnoticed, unchallenged. Inside the gloomy porch he stops – about fifty yards away from him, Mrs Lees negotiates the gate to the churchyard with bicycle in tow. As Davy slips into the darkness at the side of the church he hears her call out after him.

'Absolutely nothing to worry about, vicar. Thought it was stolen, that's all. Silly, really –'

He is inside the lean-to at the side of the church. He is inside the open structure that houses the nativity tableau with its shop window dummies and stuffed farmyard animals and accessories appropriate to a manger environment. Crouching low behind the bales of straw, Davy hears the tell-tale clicking of a bicycle's wheels or spokes as it approaches the dimly lit outhouse and its thicket of shadows.

'Vicar?' Mrs Lees calls out. 'Come in, please, vicar. Over –'

He daren't take a peek. Has she given up yet? Soon he hears the sound of the bicycle as Mrs Lees makes her way back towards the porch and the doors of the church. As Davy gets up, he finds himself at the centre of the nativity scene. He is the fourth wise man – the one whose role the history books and commentators have chosen to ignore across the years although, in truth, he is every bit as capable of wonder as the other three. Look out – Davy has only gone and knocked the paraffin lamp that hangs from a roof timber above the crib. Now the shadows really get going and the assembled players leer at Davy – notably the Virgin Mary, who has a bone to pick with him regarding his waltzing technique and his conduct unbecoming. Never mind. Not to worry. Davy knows what he has come here to do. Without further delay he peels back the swaddling clothes that dress the crib to uncover completely a children's doll of the plastic kind with nylon hair cut short like a boy's below a halo, or headband, of gold tinsel. This must be a top-of-the-range product, Davy thinks – a superior model. When he raises it up and tilts it experimentally this way and that, the doll's eyelids open and close cleverly, fringed by darkly luxuriant lashes that someone has set out rather crudely to trim to within the bounds of a decent masculinity. Yes, he will take the deluxe dolly from the crib. Yes, he will steal the plastic Jesus. He is anxious, of course, about the whole project. On an anxiety scale of one to ten he is at twenty. Nevertheless, he is resolved to destroy himself, or his chances of happiness. He has an opportunity here and now to return the doll to the crib before rejoining the choir, but he doesn't accept it. As he nears the gate, he hears them strike up The Holly And The Ivy with tremendous gusto.

In the rain-soaked streets Davy passes through puddles of red, green and gold light, wearing a smile of fortune. He fails to acknowledge, without actively ignoring it, the Saturday night crowd, or its rougher element, either entering or leaving the less salubrious of two public houses in the village. Up ahead, the picture house is emptying out in twos – see how the couples stream past Davy, belting coats, donning hats, without noticing him. And he doesn't see them either. That is because he is in a world of his own. The publicity shots advertising The Night of the Hunter, upcoming attraction, are wasted on him.

Then, quite unexpectedly, Davy finds his progress is blocked by two young people. Murdo is with Zibby on the glistening pavement in front of him. They are arm in arm – that is the key physical discovery Davy makes at this time. And although he can see they are laughing at him, he can't actually hear them. He is watching a silent movie, a film whose soundtrack has been erased for the public good. Look – Murdo and Zibby are busy making a physical discovery of their own. They are pointing out something amusing. When he glances down, Davy sees his pullover is stretched tightly over a pregnant bulge. This is all very entertaining, he allows in a faraway fashion, sleepwalking past his classmates and wearing his secret smile for anyone to see.

The light burns behind the net curtain at the window of Adam Boyd's caravan as Davy raps on the glass. Almost immediately, the door opens to reveal Rachel. She looks much as she did the last time, got up as she is once again in Adam's coat at the top of the steps and framed by the doorway. This time, however, she has a hunting rifle cradled in her arms.

'Pop –' Rachel says, taking aim woozily at the linen-clad bundle Davy carries under his arm. 'Bang, bang – you're dead.' Has she been drinking? Of course she has, Davy decides. After all, he knows the symptoms. Has she been crying? Most probably, he tells himself as part of a rapid summary of available evidence. 'What's that you've got there, Davy? Is it a gift – a peace offering, mebbe – for Rachel from Mrs James?' Now she is raving, surely. 'Oh, aye – Mrs James, the famous war widow. Butter won't melt in her mouth.' And here it looks to Davy as if the young woman in front of him makes up her mind to hurt herself the more, or to debase herself further, or to feel whatever it is she has been feeling to a greater degree, the greatest degree possible. She lowers the rifle. When she opens Adam's coat Davy can see she is naked beneath it. In concluding he knows what she wants him to do he is wrong, wide of the mark. He is too young for that, and this Rachel understands clearly because, although she is generally unschooled, she knows the difference between right and wrong. 'What's the matter, funny man?' she winds up bitterly. 'Cat got your tongue?'

He is sad in that moment. Although he lacks personal experience of these things, he can see very well that Rachel is lovely, and this loveliness, which he regards as having little practical usefulness to him, makes him sad. He wants to step back from the caravan and its punishing light, but something tells him he must stand his ground – this he does for her sake, not his. 'Where's Adam?' he asks finally, but hardly for the first time. All his life, it seems, he has been asking the same old question. Now he is ready. Tonight, he is ready to tell Adam something important, something special and true. 'There's something I need to tell him,' he adds, as though he wants to make this a matter of public citation.

Rachel nods, drawing her coat tightly around her. 'Funny thing, that,' she says. 'There's something he needs to tell you, too.'

'Oh?' Davy says. 'What's that?'

'Call it women's intuition,' Rachel says, shrugging as if to retreat notionally from an earlier stated position.

'Where is he, then?'

'You really don't get it, do you? You must be the only bugger who doesn't.'

'Is he up at the hotel?'

'You're not even close. You have a think about it, Davy – see if you can. Let's just say he's up a ladder somewhere on the other side of the lake for to fix an old friend's leaking roof.'

CHAPTER ELEVEN
The Fabric of the Night

DAVY RUNS ALONG THE SHORE OF THE MOONLIT LAKE, his white bundle tucked tightly under his arm. If he looks to his left he can see, far away across the frozen expanse, the lights of Müller's Christmas tree on the lawn of the Abercrombie Hotel. In front of him his breath comes and goes in silver clouds. As he runs, his shoes crunch through the moustache of thinner ice at the water's edge. Below the surface of the lake the eye of a pike flashes and is gone, but Davy doesn't see this at all. How could he hope to register the eye of a fish when his mind is so taken up with fast-moving events?

Now the sock on his right foot – the foot that wears the damaged shoe – is soaked right through with water from the lake, but this is no impediment to a fit young man with multiple issues to confront. As he runs, Davy thinks about the three different things that compete urgently for his attention. Although they are clearly different, these things are somehow connected, the youth decides, just as sky, lake and shore are at once separate and conjoined. The first thing is this – the bundle under Davy's arm, a cargo which comprises a plastic doll bound in linen, is increasingly burdensome to him. His theft of the infant Jesus from the village nativity scene strikes him now as so shocking and absurd as to be literally beyond comprehension. Stop – an unhappy youth is bent over at the edge of a lake for the purpose of retching. When he looks up at the moon a possible solution occurs to Davy. He might retrace his steps all the way back to the lean-to at the side of the church in order to restore the purloined Jesus to its crib – no questions asked, no harm done, no laws of normal, rational conduct broken, nay, smashed into a thousand pieces and scattered on the wind. Is it feasible at this late stage? Is it viable as a plan? Oh, Davy doesn't care right now about Murdo and Zibby and his fast-dwindling chances of bagging the bank manager's daughter for his Scramble partner. This second nagging concern is as almost nothing compared to the dread business of the doll. But there are at least two obstacles or flaws associated with the idea of returning to the church in order to undo what has been done. The first envisages very simply the potential for apprehension. To be caught in the act of returning stolen goods is almost as bad as being caught stealing them – almost, but not *quite*, as bad, Davy decides in an agony of circumspection. All the while he works hard to keep at bay the third factor or force, which is also the second obstacle to his recovery plan. It is all about something the lovely Rachel let slip concerning Adam half a lifetime ago. What was it that Rachel said once upon a time on the southern shore of the lake? *There's something he needs to tell you, too.* No point in pretending Davy struggles to recall Rachel's words. These words he carries flagrantly about his person like a botched tattoo. These words are easily the most significant items to undergo scrutiny as part of his unfolding programme of priority actions. They are the reason Davy fails hopelessly to make the right call in relation to the stolen Jesus. Now he is running again, ironic and challenging bundle under his arm. To go on is as difficult as to go back. To go back is as dangerous as to go on. Up ahead is the old stone house on the northern shore of the lake. Up ahead lies an important discovery – of this the youth is one hundred per cent certain. Whatever it is, it won't wait.

He is at the gate, the broken gate that leans – has always leaned – drunkenly on its hinges. No lights at all inside the house – not even at the Christmas tree in the bay window facing the lake. What does that mean? It means nothing. Not yet. First Davy dumps his white parcel in the big pram at the side of the house. What a relief to be without that symbolical freight at last. At the other side of the house the youth finds what he is looking for. Here it is that, out of sight of the snooping moon, Adam's trusty ladder climbs skywards on its way to the eaves and the roof. Close to the ladder, below the apex of the gable, the light glimmers dimly at the upstairs window belonging to Lydia's bedroom.

Now his heartbeat, not yet recovered from his lakeside exertions, accelerates once again. Discarding his shoes noiselessly, Davy begins to climb Adam's ladder, pressing his frame against its frame, pausing after each step to review the consequences, such as these might be, of his upward progress. Nothing. Not a peep anywhere in the world until the very top. It is as if they have held off suddenly in order to listen out for witnesses, for interlopers, in the night. Now they have resumed their activity, very physical both in sound and nature it seems to Davy at the window with its louvres not quite closed. What does he see inside the room? He sees his mother on an unmade bed with, on either side of it, the lighted candles. Lydia is kneeling on a distressed surface, both hands on the iron bedstead in front of her, while Adam fucks her violently in line with their respective needs or their expectations of the event. The thing is this – Adam hasn't even bothered to undress in order to play his part. That is what hits Davy hardest at the top of a ladder out of sight of the moon at the side of the noble house on the shore of the lake. Although he is shocked, he is not helpless in the face of the unimagined truth. Indeed, there is a terrible rightness, it seems to him, about current affairs – it occurs to the youth he is only now waking up from a lifetime of slumber. No, his chief concern here and now is essentially practical or logistical – how on earth will he get back down Adam's ladder without rending the fabric of the night?

Lydia and Adam lie side by side on the unmade bed – one is almost naked, the other fully clothed. Although they are close to each other they are not actually touching in any way or at any point. One of two smoking candles has recently gone out beside Lydia's bed, but, if anything, the shadows, such as exist in this simply furnished room, are more organised and prominent now, associated as they are with a single light source.

'Aren't you cold?' Adam says without stirring.

'No,' Lydia tells him, easing a robe from underneath her before getting up and moving to the shuttered window.

'You're imagining things,' Adam tells her.

'I only wish I could,' she says, peering through the wooden slats towards a glimpse of lake. 'I know what I heard,' she adds, transfixed for a moment by the still beauty of the night. 'There's someone out there. Someone or something –'

'There's rivers with fish in them out there,' Adam says, swinging his legs off the bed. 'You're hearing things, Lydia. Perhaps you need a good drink in you.'

'This can't happen again,' she tells him. 'It won't happen again.'

'A boy needs a father,' he says unexpectedly – unexpectedly, that is, as far as Lydia is concerned.

'What is that to you?' she asks him.

'Have I not been a father to him as best I can?'

'I don't altogether follow your meaning, sir.'

'No? Is it not you who would keep the father from the son?'

78

She stands in front of the window looking back towards the bed. He sits on the edge of the bed facing away from her towards the wall. 'Ah,' she says after a minor delay. After that comes a further short hiatus. 'Ah,' she says again, nodding slowly for her own benefit.

'Why would you choose not to speak to me about it for all this time?' he says. 'What kind of person does that, Lydia? What kind of woman does that?'

'A mother,' she says.

'You don't think me good enough, I suppose,' Adam says. 'Good enough, though, to bed you once a year under a harvest moon – is that it?' There is no anger in his voice – he has been over this ground so often inside his head and on a lonely hillside at dawn. 'How could you think I wouldn't know my own boy?' he goes on quietly. 'I have been afraid to touch him. I have been afraid to love him. At all times these small things are subject to your permission, are they not, Mrs James? And what of Davy? Doesn't he deserve to hear the truth?'

There is no point in sharing her feelings with him. The present scene is about Adam and Davy – she understands this well enough. And that is all right. That is what she has been waiting for, is it not? 'You know Davy is a special kind of boy,' she says, sitting down on the edge of the bed. Now they are back to back with their shadows leaning over them.

'Yes,' Adam says in his own time. 'Why do you think I have been afraid to touch the lad? Why do you think I have been afraid to love him as I should?'

'What will you do now?' she asks him after considering what he has just told her. Only a man would say such things, she tells herself. Only a man could say these things.

'I don't rightly know,' he says. 'I might just as easily ask you the same question. What will you do now, Lydia?'

She has a powerful desire to open the shutters, and the window itself, on her portion of lake and sky. 'You should go home now,' she tells Adam instead. 'Davy will be back soon from choir practice.'

'Yes, I'll go home,' he says. 'But first you must promise me you'll tell Davy what he should know – tonight. Otherwise, I swear I'll tell him myself in the morning.'

'Ah, yes, promises,' she murmurs as if he has already left her. 'I hardly trust them any more – especially when they're my own.' Now she hears the door to the house close softly, or considerately, behind him. Soon there comes the sound of the ladder being lowered from the side of the house. Is it over? Or is it just beginning? Lydia decides it must be both, and that is all right with her. To float momentarily between these two fateful positions strikes her as heaven on earth. She gets up from the bed, gliding barefoot across the room in order to shut the door, then rights the black and white photograph of her late husband on the dresser. She has her hip flask inside the drawer, of course, but she eschews this with barely a passing thought.

Standing at the open window, she has no sense of the cold. Is it a kind of strength or an absence of feeling that protects her from the night, from this one before all others? Looking out at the moonstruck scene she has the image inside her head of a young man and a young woman running hand in hand from their picnic and looking back at someone or something. The young man wears full dress uniform – the young woman is in a summer skirt having a lovely floral pattern. That picnic, too, was abandoned, Lydia reminds herself sadly at the window of the old stone house beside the lake. Everything changes, but everything stays the same. There are rivers with fish in them out there, Adam says, and this is plainly true. There is *someone* out there, Lydia insists – otherwise the night would be too lonely for words.

CHAPTER TWELVE
Plenty

THERE IS NOWHERE HE CAN REASONABLY take himself off to on this night of revelations. After he climbs down Adam's ladder, Davy has nowhere to go. He can't go home – not yet, at least. Any return to the caravan across the lake he rules out. To see Rachel again on such a night is one thing – to risk confronting Adam, powerful lover of women, is quite another. He could go back to the church, of course, and confess his sins and seek forgiveness there at any time, but this, too, strikes the youth as an inferior option under the circumstances – circumstances that have to do with the recent theft from the church nativity scene of its star attraction. There is no going back from here, Davy decides, outlaw status confirmed by his new homelessness, as he sits, knees drawn up to his chin and tucked inside his jumper, on the shore of the lake opposite the Abercrombie Hotel. Gazing fondly at the lights of Müller's famous Christmas tree he starts singing The Holly And The Ivy softly and sweetly in a calm, clear voice which has no official register but which sits comfortably in a realm not too far from tenor. At length he begins to shake, just a little at first, then with increasing intent, so that soon he is curled up in a ball, rocking back and forth on the shingle, and moaning audibly.

So it is that Adam Boyd, returning from the stone house to his caravan on an old bicycle and with his trusty ladder on his shoulder, first hears and then sees the youth struck down by moonlight at the edge of the water not far from the lakeside road. Adam's initial urge is quite natural. He wants very much to throw down his ladder and his bicycle and to run to the water in order to rescue his boy from the depths of his evident distress. He doesn't do that. It wouldn't be right – not tonight, not after what the youth has witnessed from the top of a ladder outside a bedroom window. Is it reasonable to assume such harsh witness has taken place? Adam thinks so. As he pedals his bicycle ever onwards towards the village his heart cries out in savage oaths and brutal imprecations behind his ribcage. It is wrong that it should unfold like this. It is unfair that it should come to this, Adam decides, ambushed and overwhelmed suddenly by a violent emotion for which he is ill prepared. Now there is no question about what to do. The gamekeeper-cum-handyman throws down his ladder and his bicycle and runs and runs, but when he gets to the place where the moon slips ashore there is no sign of the unhappy youth.

A match flares in a dark bedroom. Where are you now, moon? Davy lights a candle stub on his bedside table and drops the match into a saucer. As he lies back on the upright bolster, one hand is behind his head, the other holds a linen parcel to his chest. Not far away at the end of a short corridor, Lydia sits at her dressing table in her robe, confronting her reflection in the mirror as she brushes her hair out like a woman in a poem and prepares herself for what must happen. Soon she hears it – the sound of a harmonica emanating tentatively from her son's room. Oh, my – it must be sixteen years or more since she last heard the sound of that particular musical instrument. Now the mother rises from her stool and steps out onto the landing.

She is outside her room – he knows that. She will answer his call – he knows that too. Sitting on the edge of his bed beside the candle,

Davy plays a rising scale on an old mouth organ taken from the large square biscuit tin on his knee. Now he places the harmonica on the bedside table. From the biscuit tin he takes a pack of playing cards, pornographic in a harmless way, and fans these out, picture side up, on the blanket beside him. After he has reviewed these coy images according to a set formula, he gathers up the cards and stacks them neatly on the table beside the mouth organ. Next from the tin is an ancient pack of cigarettes, which Davy duly opens to reveal a single half-smoked relic. He positions the cigarette packet carefully on the bedside table along with a small black prayer book fished from the tin. Finally, he props a hand-coloured photograph of a young officer in uniform against the wall at the back of his shrine. Now he is ready. He places the last cigarette between his lips, lights it from the candle, draws on it once, and directs the smoke upwards at the ceiling.

She knocks quietly at his door and calls out his name. No reply. When she opens the door he is stretched out fully clothed on the bed with his back to the landing. 'Can I come in?' she says. No response. As she enters the room she registers the faint smell of cigarette smoke and the icy draught from the open window. There is a curious white parcel beside the bolster on the bed, but she ignores this in favour of a clutch of items grouped thematically and reverentially around the candle on the nightstand. Party to this miscellany is what looks like an old photograph, lying face down, which Lydia would love to turn over, but to do so would mean penetrating Davy's room more deeply than she might want or choose. She lowers the window a little. Then she passes sideways between Davy's prone form and the wall on her way to the candle and the photograph. His fist is clenched – she sees that. There is just enough room to sit down on the bed next to his torso, which she now does. After she has turned the photograph over she reaches out behind to touch his clenched fist, but he snatches it away as if he has been burned or scalded. 'How was choir practice tonight?' she asks finally, because this is how she has planned it.

After a short time she stops waiting for an answer. As she studies the photograph in her hand she starts to recollect. As she remembers she begins to speak. 'They were all good men, he used to say. Boys, mostly, they were, with soft beards. I saw them. Not an idea in their heads, most of them, except about what they would do after. After what? After singing patriotic songs and blowing each other's brains out, I suppose. And Johnny intends to be a pig farmer. And Tommy wants to be a schoolmaster and write poems about the way it should be. Or the way it should have been. As for Scott Edward James, he just wants to get it over with – to come home and jump into the lake hand in hand with his young bride. We swam in the lake together almost every day, Davy. I was not yet twenty. Right up until the end of September we swam in it. Nights were warm back then. Don't ask me why. When he went away again, I swam on my own. That's what I did. And waited for him to come back.' Here she breathes in deeply and exhales slowly and props the photograph against the wall behind the candle next to the other items taken from Davy's tin. 'I think you would have liked him,' she says, matter-of-fact now, as if to bring the curtain down on her little speech. 'Everyone did – perhaps because he never liked himself that much. He never loved himself too much. He was a fast learner – like you. He was a good swimmer – like you.'

'What about Adam?' Davy says without stirring at all behind her back.

Ah, she thinks. Now it begins and ends. 'You can be sure Adam played his part too –' she says. 'Before he came home. They had to return him, damaged, just as the summer started to die sixteen years ago. But he played his part – you can be certain of that. Nothing to do with tanks or guns or rifles. Funny to think of it looking back now

– Adam's war was at sea.' To her it is less than funny looking back. The familiar names inscribed on a war memorial – they scroll before her again in alphabetical order. 'Didn't you ask him about it?' she says. In her head she has an ideal picture, which she rejects, of a man and a boy discussing a war, or a theatre of war, with the aid of sketch maps and little ships and toy soldiers. 'He hasn't mentioned it at all?' she enquires now of the young man lying as still as a dead dog behind her on the bed. 'No, of course not. They never do.'

'I didn't go to choir practice tonight,' Davy takes up at last.

'I know,' Lydia says.

'I came home,' Davy says.

'I know,' she says. 'What did you see?'

'I saw plenty,' he says.

'What did you see?' she asks him again.

'Please,' he says.

'Tell me –' she says. 'What did you see?'

'I saw Adam fuck you – right hard. You had your hands on the frame of the bed.'

'I had my hands on the bedstead. That's right, Davy.'

'Are you happy now?' he asks her.

'Thank you,' she says.

'I'm not bothered,' he says. 'Why should I be? It's none of my business.'

'Ah, but it is your business,' Lydia says. 'It most certainly is that, because Adam is your father. Are you listening, Davy? Forget the officer in the photographs. Adam Boyd is your real father – I mean your blood father. Didn't you hear me say it just now? *Sixteen years.*' Here, she reaches out blindly behind her and squeezes a part of him – any part of him – and rises from the bed in order to escape. At the door she hesitates. She has planned to say something obvious along the lines of *let's discuss it in the morning*. 'You are more precious to me now, tonight, than ever,' she says instead, before stepping into the darkness of the landing.

Much later, long after she has left him, Davy opens his clenched fist by the dying light of the candle. Is it still there, the last stub? The last cigarette stub is in the palm of his hand, together with an angry red welt. Davy places the stub carefully on the bedside table, blows out the guttering candle and rolls over. That is when he comes face to face with the fact of his linen-clad parcel. He is ready to ditch the thing. He is set to cast his bundle at the night when he changes tack abruptly in response to a novel feeling – a real turn-up for the books, this, he allows. What might this sentiment amount to if not a tender and near blasphemous identification with the legendary outsider, the martyr king? Within a very short time Davy James is fitfully asleep, the infant son of God drawn in close beneath a coarse wool blanket, and dreaming a broken dream of rivers, hills and lakes full of fishes.

PART THIRD
Jesus Christ is Missing

CHAPTER THIRTEEN
Articles of Faith

I NEVER ACTED IMPROPERLY TOWARDS DAVY. That would have changed everything. That would have destroyed everything. I have never regretted the scrupulous correctness with which I conducted my waking relations with the disaffected youth – he was, after all, a minor. What happened in my dreams was, as I have said already, a different story.

'How come you never tried to touch me when we were alone?' he once asked me.

That was two years later, when Davy was preparing to leave our village for good. At the time of the events described here I had only limited opportunity to come closer to him in any meaningful sense. This was in the period shortly before the Christmas break, and I was yet to take up my new post teaching Latin at the village school. Our upstanding community was greatly exercised in those days by the theft from the church nativity scene of the infant Jesus, this object of seasonal worship having the improvised form of a plastic doll (the gift of old man Murphy's niece), by a person or persons unknown. To say this base episode was marked by a goodly amount of private wailing and public breast beating would be to understate its impact. For several weeks our village was under editorial siege as journalists from miles around came to gauge the moral temperature of the affair in the context of beleaguered family values and against an auditory backdrop of gnashing teeth.

Then one day Davy asked if he could see me. That was all he wrote, some few short words plus a question mark scribbled above a time and place on a ruled page torn from an exercise book and hand delivered to the bursar's office in an envelope with my name on it. This urgent and compelling message he had signed rather formally using both his names. Even without the names I would have known right away who had sent it.

We met next morning at the old boathouse that clings, ruined and forgotten, to the margin of the lake at its northwestern extremity and within the bounds of a shallow inlet. In this backwater it is still possible to picture a lost world of addict poets, artists in watercolour, doomed lovers, heretical preachers and wandering fools. Here, in an arboreal departure from evergreen standards, the dense growth of the hillside descends to the water's edge in deciduous species whose names I have yet to learn. So it was that the trees of the lake, devoid of leaf cover at the nadir of the year, lent to the site an aura of longing that was irresistible to me as I approached from the village, limping freely and without, as it were, any impediment. I never suppressed or disguised my disability, or my deformity, for Davy's sake or in his presence. There was no need for this – his feelings towards me were subject at all times to a fastidious physical distaste that had as much to do with his acute sense of self as anything else.

He was already there – I knew he would be. He was waiting for me in the profound shade of the boathouse with the slushy tide rising up through unsound planks around his infamous shoes. Without his school uniform he looked different, which is to say vulnerable and alone, to my way of thinking, my eyes growing accustomed gradually to the gloom. He had on a navy blue donkey jacket, which I hadn't seen before and which was too long in the sleeve – a cast-off or hand-me-down or something once fine that had languished unnoticed at the back of a wardrobe – so that the effect was both comic and tragic. Slung over his shoulder in an attempt at relaxed informality was a bulging duffel bag with rope straps.

'Are you all right?' I asked him straight away. That he wasn't all right was perfectly plain to me. He had lost weight – not around the body, so I judged, where he had always been rabbit-lean, but around the neck and face, where his eyes, slightly sunken, had taken on a fixed or staring quality (haunted is too strong and too obvious a word in this context). It was true he was more handsome than ever – or, rather, he would have been, without the unflattering leer that had current possession of his mouth. Then it came to me, or it occurred to me for the first time as a realistic possibility. He was out to test me – not to entrap me or compromise me as such, but to tempt me there and then with the adolescent body beneath the jacket. Was I right? If so, my reluctance or failure to act would have been a reversal for the youth. I had always assumed Davy understood my interest in him went beyond the pedagogical scope and reach of conjugation or declension. Of course he understood this. That is why he despised me from the start. At the same time, it was a truth or a given between us that the youth's distaste for me was reflexive and self-referential. Quite simply, he recognised something of himself in my deformed body and my embittered soul and, naturally enough, he didn't like what he saw. For me it is an article of faith that Davy will someday change his mind about us. It is a *sine qua non* of my meagre investment in happiness that this brave and beautiful boy will one day be me and I him. How else will I be saved?

'Like icebergs in a tropic sea –' he announced, circumventing my initial enquiry as to his wellbeing while taking a step towards me

91

on the treacherous decking. I didn't tell him about my dream of last night. I didn't want to make matters worse for Davy at a time when the things that most troubled him were coming to a type of head. In this latest dream he careered pell-mell through a sun-splashed wood. I had the sense the young man was running for his life – someone or something was out to get him. A shot rang out – an awful noise rolled from hill to hill and filled the valley below. Now the stag was running for its life, shafts of arrows protruding from its neck and back. First it stumbled, then it slowed just a little as if to ask *what have I done to merit this outcome?* Up ahead was the lake in high summer. It hadn't existed before, but now it made itself known to the crazed deer as an ocean of refuge on the outskirts of heaven. For an interval the beast lurched on, propelled beyond death by its own powerful momentum, before crashing into the shallow water out of sight of the dream. What good would it do to share any or all of this with Davy? How could I make him view the whole silly thing as a subliminal snapshot of my flight from intimacy? The downed deer – to me it stood for desire.

'Like moose's antlers on a flea –' I came back inside the gloomy boathouse, taking up the old nonsense rhyme beloved of, and passed down by, Latin teachers from here to China, my thoughts tuned now to the pitch of absurdity.

'Like salt and salad cream with tea –'

'Are adjectives that don't agree.' What was he up to? Was he still testing a quality in me – if not hunger then loyalty? I didn't have to wait long to find out. First, he gave a little shrug as if to say all this meant nothing to him. Then he swung his duffel bag to the decking, loosened the bag at the neck, and produced for my benefit a plastic doll currently the subject of a countywide search. Now I got it. Now I understood. I was to be complicit. I was to be Davy's confessor. It was a test, all right. It was a test of loyalty if ever I saw one.

'Why?' I managed after a second or two of introspection. At this time my imagination threw up an extraordinary impression of Davy posing for the press contingent in the much-photographed outhouse at the side of the church. Pouf! Pouf! Pouf! Three flashbulbs went off, fixing Davy forever at the head of a biblical gang of desperadoes. Just as strange – a rogue shaft of sunlight penetrated the boathouse roof in that moment, scattering birds in the rafters and illuminating with the effect of a stage spotlight the very place from which Davy had just moved. It was as though he had seen the sunlight coming and elected at the last minute to spurn it. All this paraded before me in a short space of time. And there was something else. An abstract scenario presented itself to me in outline form – it had everything to do with the test. According to the terms of this mental sketch I would threaten to expose Davy as a Jesus abductor after which Davy would threaten to make a claim of impropriety against me – the setting a deserted boathouse, the boy's word against mine. Such an ugly *quid pro quo* had no place in our dealings with each other, it seemed to me. As for what Davy was thinking as the maverick sunlight edged him with gold – it turned out I needn't have worried on that score. It transpired he was even less interested in my destiny than I had led myself to believe. 'Why?' I repeated then because he had thus far failed to respond to my original enquiry. Regarding the plastic doll – I observed now with something like horror it had one arm missing as it glowed supernaturally in the returning gloom.

'I don't know why,' Davy said finally, shrugging all over again. 'You tell me –'

I have never asked for more than my fair portion in life. I only ever wanted others to meet me half way. With the delinquent doll cradled awkwardly in his arms and his head cocked truculently to one side, Davy confronted me like a young offender expecting to be sent down. It was what he wanted. He wanted me to judge him as harshly as possible and to punish him to the fullest extent of whatever law I cared to invoke. Immediately I resolved to do neither of those things. As the idea came to me of making Davy the reluctant hero of his own story in prose I began to laugh – a little crazily, perhaps – at the miraculous doll, the mystery of the manger, and the world. What I had glimpsed was nothing less than my own salvation at the hands of the troubled youth who stood before me. This young man would, through the fateful exercise of thought and action, unchain my soul. I laughed – yes, I did. Soon Davy was laughing, a little madly, too.

'Have the police been to see you yet?' I asked him.

'Last night –' he said. 'But they won't get very far without this little beauty, will they?' And here he began to rock the amputee Jesus figure back and forth solicitously in his arms.

CHAPTER FOURTEEN
A Few Small Items of Housekeeping

IN THE CARAVAN IN THE FIELD adjacent to the Abercrombie Hotel, Adam lies behind Rachel on the narrow divan that takes up much of the interior. It is mid-morning on Sunday, and two competing sets of church bells coming from this and that side of the village clash evangelically in the smoke-rich air above the shore of the lake.

'Do you do it the same way with her?' Rachel asks just as Adam begins to stroke her long red hair from behind. On the one hand she seeks reassurance. On the other she doesn't really care. She is a free spirit she tells herself for the umpteenth time. She may go away again for a long period. She may go to Wigan to stay with her older sister who is a nurse. She may travel to the Smoke to seek her fortune. She may leave and never return. She may do any combination of these things, or she may do none of them, depending on how things turn out later in relation to what is uppermost in her mind right now.

'Don't be daft,' Adam says mechanically. As a matter of fact, it is as Rachel suspects – he is not really thinking about her at all. He is thinking about Lydia James, the fully clothed Lydia, not the naked version. He is also thinking of Davy, of course. As he thinks about his son, he asks himself what steps he should be taking in his head in order to prepare for the new era that is just beginning, at all times awaiting a knocking by the boy on the caravan door.

'You only want me because I'm young,' Rachel tells him.

'Is that so terrible or wrong?' he asks her after assessing the truth or otherwise of what she has just said.

Is this it? Is this all there is? All her young life she has wanted a place to settle down, a place she can call home. Although she is not normally given to imaginative flights or leaps, she has the picture in her head of Adam Boyd grown old beside her in his caravan by the lake. 'Did you get to see Davy at all?' she asks him now, as if she can read his thoughts.

'Stop with me here, Rachel,' he says, as if he can read hers.

'He wanted to tell you something. I told him you wanted to tell him something too.'

'Did you hear what I said just now?' Adam says, drawing, or rolling, her towards him.

'How can I stop here with you unless, or until, things change?'

'Change is coming,' Adam says, sitting, or kneeling, astride her now. 'You'd better believe it –'

'The bells have stopped,' she says. 'Do you think we're too late?'

'For church?' he says, his lips brushing hers. 'I'm not sure they'd let us in there, would they?'

And now she has a chance to test him, to test his commitment to her, if such a quality exists inside his manly heart. If he cares for her at all he will be ready to share a secret thing, or a private thing, with her. That is the way it works, Rachel tells herself. That is how it is between intimate friends and close business associates. 'What was it you wanted to tell young Davy so badly?' she says, placing a hand between Adam's mouth and hers.

'I'm not sure I'm ready for that,' he says honestly, withdrawing slightly in order to consider the thing properly and from a number of angles. Yes, he is right. He is right to keep his powder dry, short term at least, even if such a course of action risks local damage. A new era is beginning, he reminds himself. In all this he is thinking actively of the boy, as indeed he must from now on.

'Ah,' Rachel says, pushing him away now. 'I thought it might be something like that.'

'Does it matter to you?' he says, rolling off her towards the cold, damp wall of the caravan.

'Not really,' she says, sitting up and drawing part of the blanket around her. 'I'm sure it's none of my business at the end of the day.' But what exactly is her business at the end, or start, of the day? There is something she badly wants to tell Adam. It seems that everyone is anxious to say something to everyone else right now. And yet no one is saying anything at all, Rachel notes. 'I'm pregnant,' she informs Adam straightforwardly, as if indicating she is hungry, or sleepy, or starting a part-time job with small children next week.

Inside the packed church the congregation listens attentively as the vicar nears the end of his sermon. This is not a large church by any stretch of the imagination, but to see it filled more or less to capacity on this and other Sunday mornings during winter suggests a market leadership over rival places of worship such as would warm, to the point of toasting, the cockles of a vicar's heart.

'And in an era of increasing licence, of widespread corruption, of proliferating temptation in our waking lives and in our innermost thoughts and desires, He remains ...'

Somewhere in the middle of this appreciative throng sits Lydia, alone to all intents and purposes in a sea of hats. Lydia's eyes wander from the vicar in his raised pulpit to alight on Davy, the youth seen imperfectly between more hats and heads, in the choir stalls below the organ pipes and beside the Christmas tree. Mrs Lees is there too.

Indeed, she sits right next to Davy. Now she turns up the final hymn, hands Davy the open book, and confirms their closeness with what looks to Lydia very much like a wink. No wonder the youth seems at a loss. Much further back from altar and action, prominent among the latecomers and sceptics in the rearmost two rows, Saunders sits alone with his eyes on the back of Lydia's head.

'… our one true sponsor and guide. Let not so-called progress blind us to that happy and eternal truth. Even as we launch the very beasts of the field into orbit above our heads we remain, every one of us, God's creatures here on earth. In the name of the Father, Son, and Holy Ghost – amen.'

The grateful congregation stirs, spiritually refreshed and morally fortified. Soon it will be time to get up and go home. Lydia explores the faces closest to her, smiling bravely at one or two she recognises. She has to turn all the way round, however, before she finds the face she is actively searching for. Yes, the bank manager is watching her in the instant her eyes pick him out at the back of the church. And suddenly it strikes Lydia as unworthy of her – her ambivalence in response to his generous attentions she comes to think of as cheap. What would she think if he wasn't, after all, reaching out to her, on a Sunday exactly like this one, with his worldly gaze?

Now the vicar is descending from the pulpit in order to address his flock less formally from in front of the red rope railings that guard the altar. 'Just before we conclude this morning, friends – a few small items of housekeeping, if I may.'

Inside the cold caravan at the side of the lake not much has changed. Adam is close to the wall, the metal wall beaded above a set height with condensation. At this time he is propped up on one elbow and regarding Rachel's back as she sits on the bed facing the door.

'But that's impossible,' Adam says in a kind of reflex action or reaction that also happens to embody his settled view.

'Impossible or not −' Rachel says. 'I'm two weeks bloody late. And I'm never late.'

Armed with his parish notices and a few handwritten notes, the vicar continues to address the faithful − and those sitting not very far away from them. 'It's a small enough thing in and of itself, I dare say, but a selfish and unseemly act nonetheless −'

In a pew at the front of the choir stalls, Davy James feels a trickle of perspiration run down the inside of his left arm in defiance of the prevailing chill.

'It is my unhappy duty to report,' continues the vicar, 'that Jesus Christ is currently absent from the nativity tableau in the outhouse directly beyond these walls.' A murmur of disapproval, challenged here and there by misguided intimations of amusement, runs from the altar to the doors and back again. Oh, good heavens − now the vicar is turning to one side in order to examine the faces of the choir. 'Dear friends −' he says. 'My dear girls and boys − it seems unlikely he *absconded* from the manger, wouldn't you agree? Since it is usual to stick to the text in such matters, we look forward to reuniting him with ox and ass as early as possible.' Oh, my word − Davy James is transfixed. Could it be the vicar is addressing him personally? What does he know? What does anybody know? 'And now we sing our last hymn, the number of which is almost certainly on the board behind me − All People That On Earth Do Dwell.'

Very soon the congregation is on its feet. This morning's closing hymn, a crowd pleaser that comes around twice each year under this roof, is in full swing. When the first verse ends the organist stops in accordance with normal practice. While Mrs Lees takes a deep and dutiful breath, Davy carries on singing. That is to say he holds the last note on his own in an obvious disregard for accepted patterns of choral conduct, his voice ringing out loud and clear until interrupted finally by the vicar's calm bellow.

'Davy James!' Silence reigns in the church. Davy closes his little black book and gives it to the astonished choir mistress standing next to him. 'Thank you, Davy,' the vicar says as the youth edges his way quickly to the end of the pew, knocking bibles to the floor as he goes. With his back to the altar he breaks into a run. Within seconds he is at the big doors – these he bursts through without breaking stride.

It is over just as abruptly as it began. As the murmuring takes up all around, Lydia is aware that every eye is on her. That is all right. That is the price she must pay for bringing a special kind of boy into a cruel world. As she works her way tidily along her pew towards the aisle, she has her eyes on a notional horizon having blue sky above it and blue sea below. Has she forgotten her gloves? That would be unfortunate under these circumstances. No, they are there, her best gloves – likewise her good handbag. Clip-clop, clip-clop – the noise of her heels on the great tiles is shocking. Outside the church there is no sign of Davy. On the pavement beyond the gate there is no sign of him. Lydia is set to flee when she hears her name called out from behind. When she turns, Saunders is right there outside the porch in front of the church doors. When he calls her name again, she has to decide whether to stay or go.

'Let me be the first to commend today's unscheduled soloist,' he says after she joins him on the flagstones in front of the doors. At that she smiles, albeit weakly, rummaging in the patent leather handbag that hangs from her arm. 'Are you all right?' Saunders asks.

'Of course,' she says. When she abandons her searches, she finds the bank manager's cigarette case is held open in anticipation of her needs. The church leavers glide past them in satisfied couples, some of them smiling indulgently at the memory of recent events. 'I don't understand,' Lydia says, drawing just once on it after Saunders has lighted her cigarette – a perfectly ordinary looking cigarette whose status or standing she confirms now as unbecoming of a woman and unsuited to the hour. 'I'm sure I don't know what came over him.'

'The holy spirit?' suggests the bank manager, locating his tone effortlessly in an ideal zone mid-way between light and shade. As he engages privately with Lydia he acknowledges publicly with a smile or a raised hand the attention of passers-by, many of them savers or borrowers. Here comes Mrs Lees, for instance, ever one step behind her cheating spouse. 'Still on for Tuesday?' Lees asks in a reference, presumably, to some official business he has with the bank manager. His wife, meanwhile, dismisses the hat Saunders raises in deference to her with a wave of her gloved hand. 'No need for that, I'm sure,' she indicates breezily. 'There's no one dead here, is there? Not yet awhile.' Having directed herself sympathetically at Lydia she goes on to squeeze the arm above the patent leather handbag. 'Super singing voice, dear,' she whispers. 'I always said so –'

At the very moment that Saunders lights a cigarette for Lydia after church, his tomboy daughter inserts a metal funnel at the fuel tank of the father's brand-new Daimler Regency saloon in the garden of their expansive house in the nicest part of the village. As she lifts up her large jerrycan, Zibby is aware of someone or something tracking furtively one way and then the other on the pavement immediately beyond the hedge.

'Is that who I think it is,' she calls out, 'or someone much more interesting? As in someone worthy of my undying regard?' First, she sets down the jerrycan. Then she leans an elbow on the car roof and waits for Davy to draw himself up behind the hedge. 'Well? I don't think I hear you –'

'Don't flatter yourself, Elvis the So-Called Pelvis,' Davy comes back scathingly. 'I just happened to be in the neighbourhood, that's all. I was just passing, wasn't I?'

Now they are all but alone with each other on the flagstones outside the church. They are like newlyweds outside the chapel on their big day – soon the vicar himself will emerge to bless them one last time.

'I have to be there,' Saunders insists, as if to amplify some recent appeal. 'I have to go, don't I? I'm the new president, for Pete's sake. But you can save me, Lydia. Please say you'll save me from all those fine, upstanding members of our community, pillars of society all, and many with smelling salts in their handbags. Say you'll come. Or would you throw me to the Women's Guild?' Here, he breaks off to raise his hat for the benefit of the Jamieson spinsters, always the last to leave church on Sunday. 'Miss Jamieson – and Miss Jamieson.'

The two biddies nod in tandem, then address Lydia animatedly in turn. 'Marvellous singing voice, my dear,' croaks the one. 'Ruddy marvellous –' the other confirms hoarsely.

'Please,' Saunders says when they are alone together once more. This time he really means it. He has promised himself he will desist – he means completely – if she fails to respond to his latest invitation to join the world. 'Or have you, perhaps, forgotten how to dance?' Here, for the first time, she detects a need in him. This is something different, something new. When she thought him frivolous, he was just being witty or amusing, she decides now, rather late in the day. When she thought him flirtatious, he was just being charming. How could she have missed it? She is about to give him her answer when he cuts across her arbitrarily, or with an uncharacteristic disregard for timing. He must be thinking of the dance. He is thinking about having to dance. 'I'm not sure I remember how to myself,' he tells Lydia, and she recognises in him for the first time something of the lost boy. Then he reverts. Nothing is beyond his confident reach. 'It is my understanding,' he says, 'that a certain Post Office worker in our village has recently got her job back.'

'Oh?' Lydia says. 'I wonder what you could possibly know about any of that?'

'I keep my ear to the ground,' Saunders says, taking her arm and drawing her closer finally. Gently he opens Lydia's gloved hand, and there they are for anyone to observe – the crushed cigarette and the scorch mark on leather.

CHAPTER FIFTEEN
The Snake in the Garden

THE NEWLY WASHED DAIMLER DRIPS onto a paved area directly in front of the house. Curled up sideways on the passenger seat as far away from him as possible, Zibby watches with a pained expression as Davy surveys the steering wheel and various levers adjacent to it with his hands raised. To Zibby, exasperated already by this whole unscripted encounter, it looks very much as though Davy cannot quite bring himself to touch anything. It is all so expensive, is it not? The characteristic perfume, all leather and wood, of the interior – it wouldn't be surprising if the sensitive youth associates this now with his historical nausea, his infamous car sickness episode. Perhaps this place, or this milieu, is simply not somewhere he belongs.

'So –' he says at last. 'Where to?' He doesn't care where, as long as it is as far away from here as possible as the crow flies. Although he stares straight ahead, eyes fixed on an oasis that glimmers from great distance, he cannot help noticing Zibby's shrug delivered at coordinates closer to home. She must be bored already, Davy thinks with a little pang he adds to his growing store of pangs. 'Paris?' he proposes hopefully. 'Rome? Monte Carlo, perhaps?' In a slight but discernible escalation of local tensions his reluctant passenger moves to hug her own arms. The cause is lost, surely, and the case closed. In the oasis up ahead, the lanterns and incense burners are all out.

'Memphis, Tennessee,' Zibby announces, sighing and twisting herself around so as to confront the road ahead. She doesn't really want to go to Memphis, of course – not today. She doesn't want to go anywhere. She has to say something, that's all. She has to choose somewhere, as in anywhere, sticking her pin in a map of the world. Otherwise, this whole thing is simply too excruciating for words.

'Very good, milady – we should be there before dawn.' He is crying a little on the inside, but it doesn't matter. As long as they are speeding forward, eating up the miles and the night side by side, he doesn't mind. There is no question now of a motel. There is only the road, and the wailing, once in a blue moon, of an oncoming truck, or the clatter to left or right of the empty boxcars strung out like a prayer across the starlit plain. 'I bet you've got a television set, too,' Davy says after a certain amount of time has elapsed.

'And a vacuum cleaner,' Zibby shoots back. 'So?'

'You think you're pretty darned special, don't you?'

'Nope.'

'Statue of Liberty coming up on the left-hand side.' He is trying to think of a landmark that fits better with their ultimate destination. 'Correction – Mississippi river glinting like a snake in the garden of good and evil.' Oh, he is well on his way to somewhere, or something, now. It is only a matter of time before he reaches the end of the line, or the rope. 'You think you're too good for me, I bet.'

'Nope, nope, and nope again. Nope with brass knobs on. Nope to the power of n –'

'But not too good for Murdo McLean – am I right?'

'What's your problem, Davy?'

'Cotton field up ahead, milady. Former slave plantation on the horizon now.'

'We went to the flicks together. Big deal.'

'I thought you were on my side, that's all. I thought we were tight. You sang me a love song once upon a time.'

'Did I? So what?'

'So, how can you be on his side, too? How can you manage to be his friend, too?'

'I don't really see how it's any of your business – but, if you must know, he makes me laugh. Murdo happens to be a funny guy.'

'And I'm not?' Of course, he understands very well he is setting himself up for a fall. To speak thus at this time is to invite ridicule or mockery. And she laughs. Zibby laughs a little, but she makes sure she stops this side of the glinting river – the river of bad breeding. She is sad about Davy. It is unfortunate for him – the way things are. But she has her own path to follow. If you were out in front would you go back to help someone who was struggling? He has his hands off the wheel now. His head he leans against the window beside him. What on earth will he say next? She can see she has hurt him with her involuntary laughter. 'Have you ever thought about what it must be like to be dead?' he asks without looking at her. This is a shock to her. What he says now is nothing like what she expected him to say. 'What if,' he goes on, 'it's like falling asleep and reliving from one minute to the next all the lies you've ever told and all the mistakes you've ever made? Only, this time you never get to wake up from the dream. Not ever. And the dream goes around and around –'

'Jeez,' Zibby says. 'Are you feeling all right?'

'Of course,' Davy says. 'Don't I look all right? I'm just saying, is all. I was just thinking, that's all.'

'Well, don't. I'm not sure it suits you.' In the silence that takes hold she recognises what she must do, or say, next. She must follow through quickly on what she has done, or said, thus far. 'Look –' she says. 'You might as well know. Murdo has asked me to partner him.'

'Ah,' he says, and this is really too small a word, or too slight an utterance, to encapsulate what he thinks of Zibby in that moment. She refers, of course, to the Scramble. She means Murdo McLean has invited her to be his female partner for the Scramble, and, if we understand the thing correctly, she has agreed to his proposal. She hasn't actually said as much. She hasn't so far confirmed in writing her intention to partner Murdo, but that is the inference we draw. How cowardly or remiss, in a funny old way, not to confirm actively for Davy's sake her acquiescence in Murdo's scheme.

'Maybe you should go now,' Zibby says. 'Dad will be back from church soon. As a matter of fact, there are one or two chores I should probably have completed by now.'

But he is not quite ready to leave her. 'I thought,' he says, 'you thought the Scramble was a waste of time. I can't see what all the fuss is about – isn't that what you said? I thought you said it was stupid, or childish, or degrading to anyone who had anything between their ears – as opposed to between their legs, I presume you meant. Don't I recall you saying something like that?'

'I think I said perhaps you should go now, Davy. Just get out of the car, please, and run along home. Who asked for your opinion, anyway? Who asked you to be here, anyway?' She is waiting for him to locate the door handle – when he doesn't do that, she opens the door on her side, gets out of the car, slams the car door shut, opens the front door of the house, and then slams that door shut behind her too. All this rapid activity is very satisfying to Davy. He pictures Zibby in the hallway or vestibule of this substantial house, a house equipped with both a television set and a vacuum cleaner, a house he has never been inside, her back to the front door, her hand on the door knob or door handle behind her, her breath coming and going a little faster than she is used to or she would like.

107

'Murdo McLean is a nasty piece of work,' he calls out, his head against the cool glass of the car window still. 'Murdo McLean is a fucking bastard, Zibby. Don't tell me you don't know what he's like.' Can she hear him? After all, he is inside a vehicle with its doors and windows closed. This car, which he used to hate, is his friend. This car, witness to certain low points of his existence, knows more about him already than most of his teachers or his classmates will ever do. 'Your boyfriend's a bully, Zibby. That's exactly what he is. And one day he's going to get his comeuppance.' What a magnificent car this really is, Davy thinks, opening the window now just for the hell of it and admiring more mindfully all the illuminated gauges beyond the steering wheel. 'You're no better than he is, Zibby Saunders. Can you hear me? I know you're listening inside your lovely big house. You think it's impressive, do you, when someone throws his weight around? You think it's clever, do you, when someone waves his dick in the air? I don't think it's clever, let me tell you. It looks like I was wrong, Zibby. Are you still listening? I so wanted to believe you were different, but you're exactly the same as all the others. I mean you're not strong enough to set yourself apart from the herd.'

Abruptly, the front door opens again just a short distance from the car. Zibby leans in the doorway with arms folded loosely beneath her small breasts. 'Have you quite finished ranting and raving?' she enquires patiently.

Now he is getting out of the car. He has plenty of things to do in life. Some of these things, such as coming to terms with who his real father is, can be visited at any time of day or night. Others are best suited to the dark. As he gets out of the car, Davy disturbs a couple of levers beside the steering wheel. This probably wouldn't matter if the keys weren't in the ignition and the dashboard lights on. At first the wipers journey smoothly enough back and forth across the still moist surface of the windscreen. Soon they begin to complain with a horrible squeal, increasingly grating on the ear. 'Good luck in the Scramble,' Davy calls out, backing away at last towards the hedge, the road, and the future. 'I mean it. I'll be rooting for you –'

It is dark. It is very dark – just the way he likes it, or wants it to be. In the ancient boathouse the air is attuned to a pattern of shrieks and sighs as the ice first grips and then releases the rotting infrastructure. Here, in the deepest recesses of the lake, where decaying vegetation has a warming role, the ice migrates locally in creeping floes. Further out, a stone's throw, say, from the remnants of the boathouse slipway and jetty, the reality, like the picture, is different. In this middle part of the inlet, a zone of only limited flow, the thicker ice is strewn with silvery branches torn from the trees above the lake and destined to languish on the desert surface until the thaw comes, if and when it comes. Beyond that lies a third zone, a hostile expanse made up of frozen continents lapped by harsher currents and criss-crossed when the moon is full, or near to it, by padding foxes bent on plotting the shortest route from one side of the world to the other.

Inside the boathouse a solitary figure moves on all fours across the treacherous terrain towards the outer limit of the structure and the open lake. In fact, Davy James is not quite alone. In the bulging duffel bag on his back he carries the hard plastic doll stolen from the village nativity tableau half a lifetime ago, or what seems like half a lifetime ago. That is not all he carries. Also inside his faithful duffel bag are several large stones or small rocks, including a more or less representative sampler tied with twine to the doll's unyielding body. It is Davy's intention to hurl the doll, with weight attached, into the air above the lake and as far from the boathouse as he can manage in such a way as to commit it for all time to a further darkness below the ice, the darkness of the unknown. Quite frankly, he never wants to clap eyes on the wretched dolly again as long as he lives. Nor is it just a practical imperative – the necessity of parting company with stolen goods in one way or another and as early as possible – that shapes his choices and drives his actions. There is something else – something that has little to do with the sheer physics of his current undertaking. Davy can't put his finger on what it all means. He only knows it means *something*. In ditching the troublesome Jesus figure he is looking to drown his confused feelings in relation to Adam Boyd, and his bitter disappointment in respect of Zibby Saunders. That is what he would tell you if he was emotionally equipped to say what is really happening in a shadowy boathouse beside a hazardous lake at dead of night. His sense of betrayal he experiences twice over. He has always looked up to Adam without understanding why, and now that he has every reason to move closer to him he finds he no longer looks up to him. Is that what this is all about? As for the Scramble – how could he have thought it was for someone like him? Anyone can see it is for other people – normal people like Zibby and Murdo.

Now he is on a mooring spit that extends in ramshackle fashion from the front of the boathouse. Is it solid enough to bear him up? In standing upright on the slimy timbers the youth understands he is focusing his weight within a limited area only. Far better, surely, to spread himself full length on the unstable platform – but how then to launch his secret and complex projectile successfully into the air above the lake? Davy stands. As he removes his duffel bag from his back, he goes through it all again in his head. There is a puzzle, or a conundrum, at the heart of his plan. The challenge, which has a lot to do with the variable thickness of the ice at this or that distance from the boathouse, is the reason why Davy has brought with him rocks and stones of different sizes and weights. The further out the envisaged entry point for the doll, the safer he will feel – but at such a remove the ice of the inlet is thicker, requiring a heavier stone to penetrate it. He could rely on a larger stone to break through with more certainty, but this would restrict his throwing range to nearer the shore, which he views as inherently riskier in terms of hiding the doll forever. The nice mutuality of these dynamic interrelationships is not lost on Davy. Unfortunately, he has neither the time nor the mental space to appreciate the thing more fully. Once again, he tells himself he should have buried the doll in a shallow grave on the hill above the lake. But then it returns to haunt him – this image of the sniffer dogs drooling and straining at the leash.

He is ready. He throws his first stone, a large pebble of medium heft, into the middle distance where it bounces on landing and then skids across the ice. Part of the problem for Davy is the rickety nature of his launch platform, which makes it difficult at all times to get the purchase necessary for a strong lob. His largest rock is next up – this he heaves just a short distance into the air above the lake but with a clear success. As the rock plunges through the ice and is gone, the youth's heart is filled with gladness. Now he is getting somewhere. It only remains to calculate a median lobbing distance matched to the middling rock already roped to the Jesus impersonator. Soon the doll itself is in the air and describing the perfect arc between doubt and faith, between triumph and disaster. Alas, there is no breakthrough as such. Why would there be? How could there be? The doll lies on its back on the ice and waves its pudgy legs and arm – its single arm – at the night sky. Just how far out is it? Twenty yards? Twenty-five? Davy is disappointed but hardly surprised at this unhappy outcome. How can he expect to find absolution so easily, given who he is and what he has done? He has two choices as he sees it. He can either get down on his knees and pray for the most precipitous thaw since records began, or he can set out on his stomach across the ice using rotting planks to distribute his weight as evenly as possible. Or, since neither option precludes the other, he could essay both, the second coming, in all logical likelihood, before the first. Soon he is gathering timbers for the most desperate mission of his young life. By the time he pulls the blanket over his head in the old house on the northern shore of the lake the first birds are singing. No sign as yet of a thaw, but in a dream of summer that visits Davy at around dawn, a plastic object catches the eye of a curious pike at the bottom of the lake.

Chapter Sixteen
In Xanadu

As Lydia reports again for work at the village Post Office after her brief period of unemployment, she hears the shutter go up with a familiar clatter at the service counter.

'Hallelujah, chuck –' declares her colleague Betty from the rear of the shop. 'It's a brand-new day in Santa's grotto. Welcome back to la-la-land –'

Soon the two women are busy franking brown paper parcels – Christmas presents by the look of them – which they drop into the voluminous mail sack behind them. There is something bracing and at the same time soothing about managing these parcels with their excitable stamps and sensible string. Every so often, having studied an address or a label, the women offer an opinion as to the contents and provenance of this or that parcel – *hand-knitted scarf from the Miss Jamiesons to the usual,* or *box of fine cigars from old man Murphy to a political crony*. These gifts represent a surprisingly narrow range of needs and desires, it strikes Lydia this year more than ever. Such a downbeat assessment of the scope and reach of human happiness – is it just a product of her limited ambition in the field to date? The point is, she decides, to make the most of what is left. We are in this whole thing together, and Christmas may be our best time yet, by the way. How odd to think of it as something comparative or provisional – as if the season to be jolly might one day be downgraded or removed from the calendar altogether.

Now the conversation behind the Post Office service counter in the half-hour before opening time turns inevitably to what might be described as gossip – gossip, but not quite idle gossip. To Lydia it is remarkable that her co-worker this morning should know anything about it. After all, she only got wind of it herself some twenty-four hours ago. We are in this whole thing together, are we not? We are all connected, surely, whether we like it or not.

'Jealous?' protests Betty. 'Little old me? Too right I'm bleeding jealous. Yes, Cinders, you shall most definitely go to the ball.' Here, she snaps her well intentioned fingers at Lydia – it seems the older woman is less engaged than she might be with the prospect at hand. 'The ball, chuck! Music and dancing, witty repartee and sparkling champagne – not my cup of tea at all.' Here, Betty hugs a package to her breast in a gesture of uninhibited fondness. 'And he's such a catch, my dear. A tad too mature for little old me, of course –'

Laughing briefly and self-consciously but happily enough, Lydia rescues the unlikely marker for romance from Betty's clutches and tosses it unceremoniously into the sack. 'Have you, perchance, taken leave of your senses?' she asks. This is the Conservative Association Christmas knees-up we're talking about – in case you hadn't noticed. Cue lecherous bores with pokers up their bottoms, and pink-haired battleaxes with dead foxes at their saggy throats. Cue interminable speeches about the role of citizenship, with mutual backslapping and self-congratulation on a gargantuan scale. What could possibly be less romantic, I ask you?'

'A girl can't have it all. At least the old codgers should be loaded. They say it's a great comfort when you wake up the next morning.'

'Betty Boothby – a little decorum, if you please.'

114

'Don't you Betty Boothby me, Lydia James. I'm just following your lead. A woman in your position has to look after her interests, I'd say. And you do have interests, don't you?'

A knock now on the window of the shop door. Is it time to open up? Lydia puts down her rubber stamp and her latest parcel – jigsaw puzzle, one thousand pieces, inspirational scene featuring tall ships under sail or similar. 'I might have,' she informs her friend, getting down from her stool with a shiver of what must be self-actualisation. Has she not put it behind her finally – the difficult business of Adam and Davy, Davy and Adam? Has she not crossed the dark ocean that ends at the shore? Yes, it is time to open up. 'I just might have at that,' she confirms, for her own edification mostly, as she approaches the door. She hasn't had a drink for hours – no, days. Funny thing – the more acute or intense the life circumstance in this new climate, the less appetite or affinity she has for the workings of the bottle.

At about mid-morning at school, in an era of mounting end-of-term fever, the class waits noisily for the history teacher to extinguish his cigarette, or knock out a pipe, in the smoke-filled staff common room on an upper floor. When Davy slams the door at the back of the class all heads turn in an interested silence. Exactly what might the poor chap try next? If that is the animated question he sees written on the foreheads of his classmates, Davy opts to brush its implications aside, vaulting instead in a disciplined manner shaped by many a gym hour onto the nearest desk. First, he takes the time and trouble to seek out Zibby. Where is she? Ah, yes – she is at her usual station towards the middle of the class. In other words, she is not too near the front, in the company of the established swots, and not too near the back, the domain, according to custom, of dolts or dunces. Is she, perhaps, a chronic hedger of bets? This Davy asks himself, not for the first time.

Oh, I say – Murdo McLean has taken up a position that locates him close enough to Zibby to be able to reach out to her in a proprietorial way with his muscular arm, which he does. There is no time to lose here. Moving swiftly now to retain the attention of the room, Davy holds up for all to see a single five pound note – that's right, the very fiver dispensed from her gilded pram by nice Mrs Lees all those days and nights ago. There is a reason, he hears her say, for everything. There is a season, Davy hears the choir mistress affirm in her certain or categorical way, for everything. Now he will address the class.

'Top of the morning, people – we thank you for your attention.' Some amusement falling short of outright derision is audibly present, but that is to be expected in these circumstances. 'Many among the ladies gathered here today will recognise this scrap of paper for what it is – five pounds sterling, Erica, if I'm not mistaken.' Several titters now, and mutterings unrestrained. 'Have you ever seen such a lovely looking thing outside the context of the Christmas stocking? That is correct – one shilling to spend every day from now until the ice melts on a local lake. Think about it for a minute and I'm sure you'll begin to acknowledge the powerful attraction that five pounds sterling can exert. Are you with me so far, Janice?'

They are not sure how to read the thing now. Their response to this fluid situation – it oscillates between fascination and contempt, these two qualities enjoying a fixed place in the way they view Davy as a peer group, as a body. With the classroom falling increasingly silent as each new second whizzes past, Murdo tightens his grip on Zibby's shoulder and whispers something in her ear, but she shrugs him off in a very public demonstration of rejection. Erica and Janice, meanwhile, enter into a state-of-the-art smirking competition with each other and anyone else who cares to join in, the two principals indulging in plenty of eyeball rolling for good measure.

None of this is lost on Davy. The subtlest modulations of tribal behaviour are as an open book to him today. 'My message to you this morning is simple, ladies,' he says, taking up where he left off while folding his banknote in plain sight and then tucking it away in a trouser pocket. 'Partner me, Davy James, in a forthcoming pram race, and five pounds in hard cash is yours to enjoy free, gratis and for nothing. Well, almost nothing. All you have to do is sit on your fanny and wave like the Queen at a few yokels lining the route.' And now it is time to home in on the target. Now it is time to home in on the prize. For has there not been some small movement within the assembly? Has there not been a shift in allegiances? 'Well, Zibby – what do you say? It's an odds-on bet, right? Thou and I – we're a shoo-in for the Scramble. Five pounds in your purse and a shot at immortality. How could we lose? I mean – how will we ever know if we don't give it a try? That's right –' he concludes, his voice trailing off finally as he reaches the end. 'How else will we get to Memphis?'

Silence now in the classroom. In the corridor on the other side of the door, Mr Aldridge takes six deep breaths, as he always does, to calm himself on the threshold of habitual unruliness.

'Get to fuck, Davy,' Murdo says with a little giggle of disbelief. 'She's with me,' he adds icily before hurling an anthology of longer poems in Davy's direction.

'No, you get to fuck, Murdo,' Zibby says, gathering up her books and then squeezing in beside sensible Janice. 'She's not with you, as a matter of fact. She's not with anyone.'

'That's very good, Davy,' Murdo hisses, shaking his head at Ted who sits in the back row with the dunces. 'See what you've only gone and done this morning?'

Now comes the sound of the door opening and closing decisively at the back of the classroom. Aldridge claps his hands rousingly three times, his papers tucked under his arm. '*Bonjour, la classe. Salvete,* boys and girls. Morning, morning –' He rescues a text book from the floor behind the door and examines it quickly as he marches towards the front of the class. 'Yours, I believe, Murdo –'

'Yes, sir. It was lost, sir. Thank you for finding it and returning it for safekeeping.'

'In Xanadu did Kubla Khan a stately pleasure-dome decree – am I right, Murdo?'

'Most definitely, sir. Can we stick to history, please, sir? I don't care very much for poetry.'

'Seventeen ninety-eight, Davy – and why are we standing on our desks today?'

'I don't know, sir. Destruction of the French fleet by Nelson at Aboukir Bay, sir.'

About an hour later, when the history lesson is itself history and the refectory tables are lunchtime busy, Davy sits in underpants and shirt on the floor of the boys' toilet with his back to the wall and his bare legs stretched out in front of him. The blood coming from his nose has long since reached his collar. The knot of his school tie is impossibly tight and small – about the size of a rowan berry, say. His blazer is almost certainly close by should he care to get up to search for it. If he slides over sideways he will be well placed to gather in his shoes and to fish his sopping trousers from the gutter of the urinal. When the door bursts open just out of sight, he rises up against the wall with clenched fists raised.

She enters the toilet with his blazer wrapped up in a ball in her arms. It would be funnier if his face wasn't smeared with blood. 'Best stay where you are for the moment,' Zibby says. 'I'll fetch you some dry trousers. No – in there,' she indicates, nodding at the cubicles and then hanging the wet blazer on a door.

'Guess what I just found?' Davy says, ignoring her ministrations for the most part while retrieving a crumpled banknote from inside his underpants and smoothing it out on his thigh.

'I expect they didn't want to get any closer than was necessary,' Zibby says. 'Can't say I blame them – can you?' Shouldn't he look awkward or foolish in his white underpants and his socks with holes in them? He should look like a victim, Zibby tells herself under the flickering strip light – but he doesn't. In fact, he looks almost at home sitting there half naked on a toilet floor. Or is that what it takes to be a victim in this story – to look more and more at home in the muck and blood? 'You think you're some kind of hero, I imagine,' she says after she has taken a good look at his body in order to assess him and to judge him. 'Is that what you think?'

'What's your hunch?' Davy asks with a hollow laugh as if he can see inside her head. 'Are you saying I like the taste of my own blood? Look – you don't have to help me,' he tells her. 'I don't want your help. I don't need your pity.' Now he waves the bloody banknote in the air between them and grins. 'Five pounds sterling, Zibby. Which means my generous offer to you still stands –'

'You don't give up, do you?' she says, laughing in spite of herself. 'Give me ten minutes – and try not to fall in love with yourself while I get there and back.'

In the caravan in the field that adjoins the hotel's lawns, Rachel fills a suitcase with her clothes and a few belongings – the items, that is, which demand, by virtue of their practical value, a role in any young woman's future. To describe Rachel's future as uncertain is to bring an entirely objective sympathy to bear on her outlook and prospects – she herself exercises a touching faith in her capacity for striking a workable deal with the forces of life in whichever town or city they are to be found. Take Wigan, for instance. She has a sister there who is a nurse, a very capable nurse. Rachel's older sister in Wigan will know what to do and how to do it. Even so, it is hard for Rachel to leave like this, without, that is, saying goodbye to the father of the child she will never have. At least young Davy is here with her at this important time. The youth has the knack or the habit of interposing himself in this or that affair at the moment it reaches its emotional high-water mark. Is that a good thing or a bad thing for Davy and the world? Rachel thinks she knows the answer. That is why the boy had better watch his step. That is why she is so fond of him. How sad to think that all the love she is capable of giving is right here in this space. It doesn't take up much room. Her love – it is caravan-sized. No, Rachel thinks – that is all right. That is perfectly OK. Let Davy have it. Let Davy have it if he wants it.

'Where are you going?' he asks, shifting sideways in the cramped interior as she closes the lid of her suitcase on the divan. Although his question is obvious it is not foolish or redundant. Davy actually wants to know the answer. In his arms he carries the nylon shopping bag that Zibby has loaned him for the purpose of ferrying home his wet trousers. As for the ill-fitting trousers he wears currently – these have been plucked, the youth imagines, with all necessary haste from the bottom drawer of a bank manager's tallboy. Why is it so dark in here? Davy badly wants to turn on the light, a bare bulb attached to a flex and fixed with black tape to the wall of the caravan. Perhaps the electrics have gone down again, Davy thinks. Or perhaps Rachel prefers it like this – with just enough light to see.

'I'm going away,' she says, reaching down to hitch up the baggy pants that are belted with string high above his waist. 'What's all this, funny man?' she asks. 'Another fancy dress party?' Here, she peels back the lapel of his blazer to reveal the bloodstains on his shirt. She makes no comment. She doesn't kiss him on the head. She doesn't tousle his hair or anything like that. She licks her thumb and wipes the last streak of blood from his chin as part of this opera of farewell.

'Say goodbye for me,' she says on the step with her back to the doorway, valise in her hand, a wrap over her arm. 'You know where he likes to be at this hour.' In front of her and all around are the dark hills – how they seem to close in on things today, Rachel thinks. Even the gloaming, so thrilling and special as a general rule, has a chilling quality this evening that makes her shiver. 'If you stick around,' she says, 'you might catch him coming down from up there somewhere. Then you can have that little chat you always promised yourselves.'

Why won't she turn around so that he can see her? Is she crying? Yes, that must be it, Davy decides. Many years from now, when he is a different person in a different place, he will wish he had stepped forward to comfort Rachel in this moment. Even though he knows the answer already he still has to pose the question. 'Are you coming back?' he asks.

After a brief interval given over to reflection she nods – this little fib she serves up for the boy's sake only. That is OK, she decides as she clip-clops down the steps of the caravan for the last time. That is just the way things are, or often have to be, between intimate friends and close business associates. 'Ta-ta, funny man,' she calls over her shoulder from the frozen field. 'Be brave.'

CHAPTER SEVENTEEN
Accommodations with the Truth

DAVY DOESN'T WAIT FOR ADAM IN THE CARAVAN after Rachel has left. He doesn't visit Adam in the gamekeeper's hut on the hillside – not for the time being at least. Instead, the youth takes to his bed for a day and two nights, supping only brownish water from the tap. He is not sick as such. He is not ill in the clinical sense. He spends a great deal of time trying not to compare or contrast the concept of Adam Boyd as a father figure with the rival concept of Scott Edward James as a father figure. What good could come of that? As a matter of fact, these unwelcome thought patterns present themselves to Davy very much as abstract constructs. When he thinks of Adam, for example, he is no longer sure how to address him, as in what to call him to his face. If he cannot get over this small procedural hurdle he is doomed – that much he accepts wretchedly as he tosses and turns under the blanket. At first his mother is worried about him. He has never been a sickly boy – not in the physical sense. After she has notified school, Lydia settles down to wait for improvements in her son's status and outlook. These must come, she tells herself, if there is to be any future at all for the two of them. Meanwhile, Davy tosses and Davy turns. At night he has the dream of the doll. In this dream, which has all the hallmarks of the recurring type, a muscular arm or a hand raises the immaculate doll up through the surface of the lake over and over again. The dream is just a dream, Davy tells himself. What unsettles him more is the idea, unworthy of his best self, that he might actually prefer the older version of what his father looks like – this construct built up faithfully over many years – to the newer one. All the while he knows it – there is no point in waiting for Adam Boyd to visit the old stone house on the northern shore of the lake. It is obvious all along to Davy's agile mind. It is for him to make the first move.

On the second day he gets up late. After wolfing down porridge made with sugar and evaporated milk followed by three soft boiled eggs with bread and jam, he sets off up the hill towards Adam's hut. No need to check on the caravan beside the Abercrombie Hotel. By this hour of the day Adam will be where he likes to be – in a zone of private mists and submerged memories. In fact, the morning murk has all but vanished by the time Davy reaches the log cabin with its door standing, or leaning, crookedly a quarter open as usual.

'Is anyone there?' he calls out, his voice an unfamiliar croak after so many hours spent in his own silent company. It is not what he would normally say in these circumstances. Normally he would say something like – *are you in there, Adam?* But today is a different sort of day, Davy concedes on the threshold of the interior gloom.

'Enter, please,' Adam calls out from inside. Again, this is different and remarkable. It is as if Adam too is uncertain about what to say and how to say it. To Davy it is as if they are level pegging, or on an equal footing, suddenly. The youth probably needs more space to work out whether or not he feels comfortable with this altered state of affairs. Right now, it is just another element of the shifting scene. He would expect to look up to Adam Boyd in the normal course of events. That is how it has always been. Now he learns to his surprise he is already inside the gamekeeper's hut. Davy doesn't recall taking the actions necessary for gaining entry to this oh-so-special place – a masculine realm of fascination and quiet horror. The stove is lit. The dead birds hang down. Seated at the rough table with his back to the door is Adam. Odd – he usually faces the door, as if in readiness to confront an attack, or in order to make the fastest possible exit at a time of crisis. What else? There is the bottle of whisky on the table alongside two small glasses. From out of sight behind Adam's body the plucked feathers of a game bird fall silently and then gather on either side of his boot. When he speaks, he sounds different – a result, no doubt, of changing priorities and acoustic variables. 'If you've got something to say to me,' he says, 'then say it.'

'Why didn't you tell me?' Davy says. He hasn't rehearsed this in any shape of form. It just presents itself quite naturally as the logical place to start.

'Because I didn't know,' Adam says. 'At least not for sure. Such a thing is best left to your mother, after all. It is not for me to call. You see that, don't you?'

'You made a proper little bastard of me. Couldn't you even wed her somewhere along the way?'

'As I say – it was your mother's call to make. Maybe she thought I wasn't good enough for her. She wanted you to be his – Scott's, I mean. That is OK. I understand that. She kept you to herself – for his sake. Perhaps she thought she'd never have to let on. Maybe she thought you'd never grow up. Perhaps she thought she'd never have to come to terms with what she is, or was – a lovely girl who had to punish herself for a moment's comfort.'

'In your arms, you mean. Did you ever love her?'

'We were young then. I loved her right here, in this very place, on the same bed you see before you now, just as summer was about to die. I read ghost stories to her, a page each day, and we talked to the birds and the animals up here on the hill. Anything to stop her crying. Because she did cry. She cried and cried, and I wanted to make her happy. And he was never coming back.'

There is a silence now during which Adam sets aside the game bird and then pours whisky into the two glasses. To Davy these small actions are like a rite, a religious activity.

'You never told me what you did in the war,' he says from just inside the door. It is as it should be. He is reluctant to approach the man whose back is still turned towards him.

'There's not much to tell,' Adam says after a pause that signals something like *we knew this one was coming*. 'I was on the convoys. You probably knew that. Not with the navy – on the merchant side.'

'I thought you told me you couldn't swim.'

'You don't have to be able to swim.' He is out there again in the darkness – a darkness of screams and smoke and oil and tiny flames on the water. He hasn't been there in such a long time. 'One night we went down hard off the coast of Ireland.'

'What happened to you?'

'I was lucky. I was picked up quickly. Many of those men – they never learned to swim. It was like a badge of honour with them, or a superstition. They didn't intend to hang around. They wanted to go straight down. If the ship went down, they planned to go straight down with her.' He stops speaking here and resumes his work on the surface of the table. He doesn't understand even now why he should feel guilty about surviving. He did nothing wrong. He can't see why he should find it so hard to get close to people – people like his own son. If he can't understand it himself, how can he expect a schoolboy to comprehend it? 'Are you satisfied now?' he asks Davy. 'Don't try to compare me with him. Don't try to compare me with some ideal thing you've cooked up in your head. That would be a mistake, so it would. And now – Rachel told me you had something important to tell me.' He has spent a good deal of time preparing for this moment. If it comes now it should come from Davy. Yes, it is down to the boy. At the same time Adam asks himself again – *is it me? Is it in me?*

'Why did she take off without saying goodbye to you?' He has a chance here, but he doesn't seize it. He has wanted to tell Adam for the longest time, but now he no longer wants to do that.

'Because I couldn't give her what she wanted or needed. I know what you're thinking. You think I only care about what's good for me. Is that what you're thinking, Davy?'

'I was thinking about what I should call you from now on. Is that so terrible?'

'Call me Adam, just as you always have done. It will take time to get used to all this. I mean for all of us. Meanwhile, try to be a big boy, Davy. Your mother needs you. She loves you – that's the most important thing. And I have loved you too. You do understand that, don't you? I have loved you too, in my way.'

'Have you, Adam? Which way is that?'

The whisky, decanted presumably to mark the transition from one state of mind to another, is left undrunk. 'Shouldn't you be at school?' Adam says, as if to conclude. 'Or is school closed? In which case it must almost be time for the chariot race of futility. Is it time for the last Scramble, Davy – a scramble for something lost that can never be found? And what would you call such a thing? Innocence, maybe? No – a dream of innocence, let's say.'

He had expected something more decisive – a reckoning of sorts, or a showdown. As he descends the hill sadly, Davy begins to see his life for what it is, or what it will become – a series of accommodations with the disappointing truth. Among the leafless trees that look down on the old boathouse and the silver lake he stops for a moment and shuts his eyes. On the count of three he opens his eyes and listens out and looks. Is it there – the arm rising up with the fabulous doll in hand? That would be something, wouldn't it? There is nothing really to hear in this place – only the creaking of rotting timbers gripped by the ice. There is nothing really to see here – only the frozen inlet still strewn with boughs and waiting for the thaw.

Chapter Eighteen
Potentiality and Reciprocity

WE ARE ALMOST AT THE SHORTEST DAY, or the longest night. We are back inside Lydia's bedroom on the upper floor of the old stone house. It is early evening – the cocktail hour, if you like. Lydia shields her eyes with her hand as she directs several bursts of hairspray from the can towards her piled-up hair. She has at some stage tucked two handkerchiefs under and around the neck of her dress to protect the fine fabric from her make-up – now she removes the handkerchiefs and considers the overall effect, or look, in the dressing table mirror. This mirror, which has judged her so severely over the years, gives nothing away as Lydia clips on first a necklace then her earrings and turns to one side and the other and back again to inspect the finished result of her careful preparations. It is not for her she does all this, of course – it is for him, the bank manager who will shortly set out to collect her in the swanky motorcar he tries not to take too much for granted (along with a television set and vacuum cleaner). Is she ready now? She reaches for the small bottle of scent that sits on the dressing table, then changes her mind. He might not like her favourite scent, she reasons. Her preferred perfume might remind him of someone, or something, he would rather not recall, Lydia cautions. She takes her dress watch from the drawer and shakes it a few times, then puts it back in the drawer. If it wasn't working the last time she removed it, why would it work now – unless it had somehow mended itself out of sight of the world? Anything is possible, Lydia assures herself, but some things are more possible than others. This awakening instinct she has for gauging the base potentiality, relative to a notional mean value, of anything and everything is a sign of her growing investment in life. That is roughly what Lydia discusses with herself as she marks the approach of her son in the corridor between bedrooms.

'See you tomorrow, I expect,' Davy says from the doorway. His trusty duffel bag is slung over his shoulder. He understands very well what this whole episode means to her. He knows what it all amounts to within their quantum of shared experience. 'Enjoy the party –'

'Thank you,' Lydia says. The novel formality they bring to their dealings with each other at this time is not necessarily a bad thing – call it a staging post, the mother reasons, on the road to new horizons of understanding. 'Enjoy yourself at Zibby's,' she offers in return.

'I get the feeling,' Davy says, 'she wants to show me some family footage of the Scramble.' How can it be lost on the mother and the son? The intensive reciprocity of what they undertake tonight, each in the company of a Saunders, has the effect of drawing them closer while at the same time setting them apart from each other. They are on parallel missions. No – they have a common mission to orientate and integrate which they pursue jointly and separately.

'Goodness –' Lydia says. 'Has the girl had a last-minute change of heart about the Scramble? I had the impression she regarded it as a waste of everyone's time.'

'I think tonight is all about background and context. I think it's about research, if that doesn't sound like a bridge too far.'

'A bridge too far? I thought Zibby said she couldn't understand what all the fuss was about.'

'I expect,' Davy says, 'she's simply hunting down a dream.'

'Really?' Lydia says. 'Which particular dream is that, I wonder?'

'The lost dream,' Davy says. 'The dream of innocence.'

'Oh,' Lydia says. 'I had no idea the Scramble had a lyrical or a philosophical side to it these days. To me it's still just a metaphor for the messy business of living.' She has set out to say *ugly*. She has set out to say the ugly business of living, but chooses otherwise. Has she broken free from the suffocating power of words and their meaning? If she can permit herself to look back it can only be because she has reached the far side. 'But you already appreciate where I'm coming from on this, Davy,' she concludes, the lightest of laughs issued here in support of her son and what he must do in order to know *everything*.

'I do hope you enjoy the dance,' he says. He is thinking she looks different tonight – not just different in that sense, got up as she is like a comparative stranger. When he looks at her, he doesn't recognise her as his mother. He sees a woman, yes – but not a mother. Maybe she will look like his mother again tomorrow, Davy thinks, stepping back finally from the doorway. When he hears her call his name he hesitates on the landing at the top of the stairs. Such a late summons – it can only signal something untoward, can it not?

She is standing in the middle of the bedroom, dressed in her best frock but without her shoes. 'How do I look?' she asks him, spinning around once for his benefit. 'Well –' she says. 'How do I look?'

'Beautiful,' he says. She is not his mother. She is a little girl, Davy decides. 'You look beautiful,' he tells her, nodding and nodding. 'I'm going now, if that's OK. I think I'll take my bicycle.'

On the expansive lawn outside the Abercrombie Hotel in the heart of the village, Müller's famous light bulbs twinkle and click in the big tree. Cars draw up at the pillars of the hotel's porch, crunching small stones, disgorging guests. Laughter and music come and go on the bitter breeze blowing in from the icy lake as the annual Conservative Association Christmas dinner dance gets underway. Now a Daimler Regency saloon stops at the porch to let out a guest before powering onwards towards the car park at the side of the hotel. Is that Lydia James who stands alone between the pillars, nodding and nodding? She looks different, that's all. No one can put his or her finger on it, but everyone agrees – she looks different tonight.

PART FOURTH
The Last Scramble

CHAPTER NINETEEN
Walking Through Fire

I DON'T SWIM. I AM NOT A SWIMMER. At all times and in all contexts I have gone out of my way to avoid sporting endeavour, organised or not, of the group variety or any other. From the outset it was my habit to denigrate or dismiss the demonstrations of physical prowess to which most boys are inclined and attached. So began a lifelong aversion to the game – to the game, and to the changing room that goes with it. To submit my crudely commissioned body in a naked, or near naked, state to the casual scrutiny of others is to walk through fire as I understand it to be. It goes without saying that swimming, the business of swimming, acknowledged widely for its positive effect on mind, body and soul, has for me been a source of horror across many a lonely year and many a dark night riven by dreams.

I was in the lake. I am not saying I was beside the lake or above the lake. I was in it. There could be no doubt about this because I was happily taking its liquid content into my mouth before expelling it in a playful stream in just the way I had seen others do on so many occasions. To say I was content in that sweet moment would be to understate the thing massively. To feel the water, summer thick and surprisingly warm, probe and flood with its current the tiny folds and recesses of my outer casing was a kind of ecstasy. I don't suppose I was swimming as such – more likely I was floating on my back and sculling myself towards the deepest part of the lake in a reckless but necessary bid to test the water, or its loyalty. Could it be trusted, after an eternity of mutual hostility, to buoy me up? No doubt my instant of doubting was my undoing. My failure of faith was the key thing. First there was a low rumble. Soon the rumble became a roar. When I lifted my head from the water, I saw a herd of deer – no, an army of deer – crash down the hillside at a heart-stopping gallop and enter the lake with a tremendous show of spray. Now there was no doubt in my mind – these deer were gunning for me. Within seconds I was below the surface with the hooves lashing and pounding the water just above my head. Then I saw the doll. The plastic doll that had so exercised the imagination of our community was drifting upwards slowly and serenely beside me. I reached out, and it was over. When we got to the surface and broke through together there was no sign of the stampeding deer. I was floating on my back again, clutching a plastic doll to my chest, and staring at the empty sky.

Where does dream end and delusion begin? For the first time in this series of interlinked visitations my alter ego was missing from the scene. That there was no glimpse of Davy within this latest narrative merely served to persuade me of his role. That he was absent on this occasion from the dream simply drew fresh attention to his case. My obsessive research in this area rapidly threw up three possibilities. First, there was the idea, satisfying enough in its own right, that Davy was represented here by the plastic doll, my buoyancy aid and chum. The next thing I knew, my explorations had widened in scope, the latest line of enquiry being defined by a desperation commensurate with my suppressed desire. Could it be that Davy was dreaming the same dreams as I was dreaming, but with a blissful disregard for any such synchronicity? And there was something else – something that stood a fighting chance of yoking the real world to the subconscious mind in free fall. If Davy was to be implicated in a meaningful way in my salvage from the depths it could only mean one thing – he was a swimmer. Was he a swimmer? When I scanned all scenarios and locations, including St Saviour's over the hill and far away, for clues or insights I drew a blank. Still, I had to know. Absurd, I admit – in my headlong rush to redemption I staked all on the toss of a coin. If Davy couldn't swim, I was cursed pure and simple. If he swam, or swam well, it was confirmation beyond peradventure to my flailing mind of his power to save me.

I didn't have to wait long to discover my fate. No need here to schedule a clandestine rendezvous with Davy in the old boathouse, or on a shingle shore in the gloaming. In fact, I bumped into him in the corridor outside the bursar's office in the dying days of the school term. When I asked him what he was doing he said it was none of my business. When I reminded him of his subscription to our joint venture in words, he told me he had been seeing Miss Montgomery about his attendance in class. I had by this time been assigned a small office – a variety of walk-in cupboard, really – on the understanding that something more generous would be made available once I had paid my teacherly dues. It was to this cubbyhole that we retired after a brief, slightly terse, exchange of pleasantries. Such awkwardness I ascribed to the stolen doll. After all, when we had last come together, Davy and I – in a ramshackle boathouse, and on the shore at near dark – the Jesus avatar had been a token of something transgressive between us. There and then I decided not to mention the doll again. As it turned out, I didn't have to.

'How's it going, anyway?' Davy said, referring here, I imagined, to our literary joint undertaking as he closed the door behind him.

'No – leave it ajar, please,' I said. 'It's going well,' I went on, this verdict issued pretty much randomly, in fact, in support of anything that registered its claim. 'It's going very well. I just wanted to ask you a question. Two questions, actually. Two questions that, for me, are interrelated. I mean – since you're here. Since we're here.'

'Shoot –' Davy said. 'But make it quick, please. I don't have all day. I have to sign up for the Scramble before an official deadline which has already passed.'

'Ah, the Scramble. I would have bet against your being remotely interested in that type of thing.'

'Then you would have lost your money, it seems. And to think I thought you knew all about me.'

'Not quite,' I said. 'Not yet. Have you been dreaming of late, Davy?' My line of attack – such a pity it made me sound like a quack or a shrink.

'No, matron,' Davy came back gravely, shaking his head.

'Nothing at all? Not even about the Scramble?'

'Oh,' he said. 'I dreamed about the you-know-what.'

'Ah,' I said, pulse quickening. 'What did you dream?'

'I dreamed I saw it rise out of the lake. Over and over again.'

'I see,' I said. I didn't see. It was too much at that time to try to work out how Davy's dream might connect with mine in a way that transcended the obvious factor of the doll in the lake. There was no mention here of the deer, singular or plural. (The truth is I had come to terms already with the inevitable – the ideal meaning of the deer, alone or in groups, was destined to elude the official record.) And yet Davy's dream thus outlined was a validation of sorts. 'Did you dump the you-know-what in the lake?' I asked him, this question arising as a natural consequence of everything else. Of course he dumped it in the lake. How else could it have popped up to save me when it did?

'Was that your second question?' he asked, arms crossed, head cocked, and with his customary quickness of mind.

'No,' I said. 'Are you a swimmer at all?' It just came out like that, in a straightforward way that belied its significance for me. 'I mean – can you swim?'

Then Davy looked at me as if I had taken leave of my senses in a windowless office in an unglamorous quarter of the school. 'Pretty much everyone,' he told me, 'can swim these days – except for sailors in the merchant marine who like to go down with their ship.' Then he changed tack. His flippant tone vanished in response, I wanted to believe, to something he saw in front of his eyes. 'Yes, I can swim –' he said. 'Since you ask. In fact, I'm a strong swimmer.' He paused there. Doubtless he could see the effect of his words on me. 'You said your two questions were interrelated,' he reminded me then. 'So, tell me, pray – how is swimming related to dreaming?'

'To me they're both substitutes, or proxies, for death,' I told him without really thinking about my answer. In point of fact I was taken up with something barely less metaphysical in that airless office, my body pressed against the wall as far away from the youth as possible. If you only *think about* getting as close as you can to someone like the young Davy James, does that make it all right? If you fail to translate thought into deed, or dream into act, does that make it OK? These questions I was obliged to commit once again to my mental jotter in a section at the back labelled unfound. At my tribunal in heaven the angels of presumptive guilt were moving already to cast me into the healing fire. 'The court thanks you,' I said. 'You may step down.'

'What if I choose not to step down, your honour?' Davy said, as if he could see what was taking place in a region behind my eyes. For a few seconds he waited with his back to the door. In this way he made himself available, not because he wanted anything to occur, but rather so that no jagged stone might be left unturned along our scrupulous pathway. That was how I chose to view it, shrinking from his presence to the maximum extent allowed by our cramped setting. At this close remove the youth smelt faintly of cigarettes, as if he had been smoking with trusted friends behind the cricket pavilion. Then it hit me – Davy had no trusted friends. All this time he was counting out the seconds inside his head. When he got to ten, he was satisfied. 'If there are no further questions –' he said, opening the door while shuffling forward to give it space. Then he was in the corridor, facing away from the tiny room and waiting for my parting shot – the one he knew must come because he had engineered it that way.

'Best of luck in the Scramble,' I said with genuine feeling. I really meant what I said. I could see it because it was my business to see it – the futile chariot race would be the culmination of Davy's journey towards, or into, himself. This passage he made on my behalf also – such was the nature of our joint venture. By his brave example Davy would make me complete, on the inside at least. And by writing the whole thing down for the world to judge I would set him free in my turn. It was no more or less than the youth deserved. The truth is that Davy changed everyone. We were all of us changed by what he did on that hill, or in the shadow of the hill, before the bulldozers of progress changed everything. And, after all, he did go on to win the Scramble, even if it wasn't in quite the way he might have expected.

CHAPTER TWENTY

The Perfume Wars

ONCE OPULENT (OR WHAT AN American might call classy) enough, the interior of the Abercrombie Hotel is today tired and a bit shabby. No doubt this venerable establishment, like so many of its important guests tonight, has a foot stuck firmly in the past. And for a manager with a commercial eye on the bottom line, things are not what they used to be in the lakeside hospitality industry. Now the cornices and mouldings of the hotel's lofty public rooms are caked with paint, and the carpet on the imposing central staircase wears increasingly thin towards the middle part of each step, this effect being most marked on the first flight where the footfall of the well-heeled is notionally at its heaviest. As he enters behind Lydia through the revolving doors of the overheated lobby, Saunders gets a whiff, comforting and sad, of meats roasting on the rack and gravy thickening in the tray. Now Müller hurries forward from a long table staffed by a troop of waiters in white and set with a great many glasses filled not quite to the brim with what might easily be Riesling or some hock equivalent brought over in bulk from the manager's native land.

'Welcome, Herr Saunders. Welcome, welcome –' enthuses the German, beaming. 'A great pleasure, indeed. And Mrs James also.' Here, the hotelier bows effusively and mops the back of his neck with a folded handkerchief. '*Willkommen, willkommen. Wunderbar –*'

'Evening, Müller,' Saunders says, peeling Lydia's coat from her shoulders with a smile on his lips. 'Try not to overdo it, old boy.'

'*Natürlich, natürlich* —' the hotel manager protests affably, turning his attention to Lydia's coat. 'May I take it, *ja*?' He snaps his fingers once in the air beside his wide neck as he gathers in the fur coat and stole. 'Almost one hundred guests here tonight,' he reveals proudly, offloading the garments on an eager assistant red faced with acne in exchange for a numbered ticket. 'Permit me to offer you a refreshing glass of something from the Rhine region of my country. Better than French, according to your Queen Victoria.'

'Nice try, Müller. Still, if it's good enough for the wine-guzzling Empress of India —'

As the hotel manager backs away, Saunders broadens his smile for Lydia and squeezes her arm. Three strides later he is at the table with its array of glasses. After he scoops up two goblets he turns and offers one to Lydia, but she shakes her head in a way he begins to recognise — a way that says she is far too taken up in the moment to countenance such an idle distraction. 'In that case —' Saunders says, breaking off to drain first one glass then the other. 'The condemned man ate a hearty breakfast. Shall we enter the lion's den?'

On the threshold of the banqueting suite they pause arm in arm to consider the scene. Along the walls on opposite sides of the room are ranged the large round dinner tables set for eight or ten. On the dance floor in the middle of the room, the guests mingle volubly with glasses in hand as the top-up waiters circulate with bottles wrapped in white linen. At one end of the suite a band plays Glenn Miller for a band leader on a raised platform hung just above head height with a banner that reads COMMUNITY, COUNTRY, CONSERVATIVE. All this happens with a powerful sense of entitlement below a wreath of cigar smoke that caps the scene and tinges the high ceiling brown.

'Love the values on show,' Saunders whispers in Lydia's ear, his intervention designed to advertise a perfectly judged intimacy for the benefit of the assembly. 'Is that lavender, or rose, or lily of the valley that wins the perfume wars raging all around the newly arrived?'

'Looks like we may finally have emptied the seven seas of all their pearls,' Lydia says, smiling graciously at complete strangers. 'It's just possible, by the way, that what you can smell is men's cologne.'

'I'm not sure that banner quite speaks for the association's new president, though,' Saunders offers. 'What do you think?'

'I think,' Lydia says, 'the new president had better do some work on his attitude and his commitment to the cause. PDQ –'

The door opens onto a spare bedroom. Zibby Saunders switches on the light as she enters this small chamber. As Davy hesitates in the doorway, Zibby indicates the one-bar electric heater that sits on the tiled hearth in front of an empty fireplace. 'We'll plug it in for a few minutes,' she says, 'before we get undressed.'

Davy drops his duffel bag behind the door, then sits on the bed and tests its bounce. 'No television set?' he says.

Zibby draws the curtains. 'Think you're on your daddy's yacht?' she says. 'Sorry – shouldn't mention daddies in any shape or form.'

In the banqueting suite at the Abercrombie Hotel, the pre-prandial drinks are going down a storm. As he charts a course through the sea of guests, Müller bows and beams and snaps his fleshy fingers at the well-scrubbed waiters. Somewhere towards the middle of this vocal throng, Lydia and Saunders find themselves in conversation with nice Mrs Lees and her cheating husband respectively.

'It's all down to self-discipline at the end of the day,' Lees says. 'Hard work never killed a man, Max – and that's a fact. Hard work and self-discipline. Plus, of course, the odd bout of exercise. A bit of how's-your-father on a Saturday night –'

As he squeezes past their little group, Müller raises his arm and taps his watch. Saunders nods in acknowledgement.

'They do say,' Mrs Lees says, 'it sucks up the dirt like nobody's business, but I'll stick with a pan and brush and my carpet sweeper, thank you very much. It's true, dear – you know exactly where you stand with a good carpet sweeper.'

Now the music stops abruptly with a crash of cymbals. From the stage a microphone booms as Müller blows on it experimentally. As Saunders draws Lydia towards him, all heads turn towards the raised platform. 'Ladies and gentlemen,' Müller begins, clearing his throat with a precise measure of self-satisfaction. 'Esteemed guests –'

In a spare bedroom at the Saunders residence, Davy and Zibby lie side by side on the bed, fully clothed and staring at the ceiling light.

'Romeo and Juliet,' Davy says.

'Juliet and Romeo,' Zibby counters.

'The King and some American woman whose name we tend not to remember,' Davy says. 'Oh – Mrs Simpson.'

'Cleopatra and Antony,' Zibby says, rising up now on one elbow and looking down on Davy. 'So, why does the man always have to come first?'

'He just does,' Davy says, shrugging and looking up at Zibby. 'A man has got to know everything. Or so Adam Boyd says.'

At the Conservative Association's Christmas dinner dance the band plays on while the guests applaud generously from four sides of the dance floor. In the middle of the clearing, and with the odd foray at this juncture or that along the north-south axis of the banqueting hall, Saunders and Lydia dance alone. Although no one quite knows why, it is a matter of historical precedent that president and partner should be in solo action at this first opportunity of the evening.

'Sorry —' Saunders says. 'I should have warned you. An obscure tradition designed to embarrass us all before we sit down to eat.'

'We can see you're embarrassed beyond words,' Lydia says, still smiling at the world.

'You're not angry with me, are you?' Saunders says. 'In a painful series of recently recurring dreams I've been made to sweep a perfect stranger off her considerable feet at this time.' Now the clapping falls away around the room. The couples take to the floor gladly or sadly or fluently or awkwardly according to their predispositions and the effect on these of Müller's wine. 'I want you to be happy,' Saunders says, once the dance is fully operational. 'No — it's a bit more active than that, isn't it? I want you to *find* happiness.'

'I know,' Lydia says. 'You think I deserve it.'

'I do this mostly for myself and the world,' he reminds her.

'I know,' she says again. 'You insist on happiness for all as a kind of civic obligation or municipal right.'

'What else is there?' he asks her.

'The past,' she says without hesitation, as if that is invariably the answer regardless of the question. 'The past, which is always right behind us, snapping at our heels —'

'We must learn to love the past,' Saunders says. 'Where on earth would we be without it?'

In a guest bedroom in this substantial house in the most desirable part of the village, Zibby and Davy kneel facing each other on the bed, shivering a little in Davy's case, and naked in the case of both of them. The ceiling light is on. The one-bar electric heater is off.

'That perfume smells nice,' Davy says. 'What kind of perfume is that?'

'I don't know,' Zibby says. 'It belonged to my mother.'

'I thought so,' Davy says. 'Can I ask you something personal?'

'I wish you would,' Zibby says.

'What did your father do in the war?'

'I'm not sure,' Zibby says. 'Something behind the scenes, I think. Something hush-hush. He doesn't talk about it.'

'They never do,' Davy says. 'Now what?'

'Now you kiss me again, of course. Or would you like me to get the book out?'

Davy hugs Zibby speculatively and kisses her briefly on the lips. 'And?' he says.

'You're supposed to use your tongue,' Zibby says. 'Where have you been for the last fifteen years?'

'Sixteen,' he informs her. 'It's almost sixteen, I think you'll find.'

Zibby holds Davy's head with both her hands, tilts her own head relative to his, and closes in slowly on his mouth. 'Well?' she says.

'Well, what?' he says.

'Don't you feel anything?' she asks. Reluctantly, she permits her axis of vision to descend from Davy's head towards his thighs. 'Oh, dear –' she says. 'I think I'm going to have to cup your balls in my hand now. That's probably in the book somewhere, by the way.'

'Actually, I feel pretty cold right now,' he says, tucking his hands under his arms.

'Yep – me too,' she says, sighing.

Then Davy takes a rug – a tartan rug he recognises from a picnic at the side of a road half a lifetime ago – from the foot of the bed and wraps it carefully around Zibby. 'I must be doing something wrong,' he says. 'Didn't I tell you? A man has got to know everything.'

'It just takes practice, silly,' Zibby says, climbing off the bed.

'Is that what Murdo says?' Davy asks. 'Sorry –' he adds almost immediately without even bothering to check his own body for signs and indicators that may prove helpful in the future. It is no surprise to him, of course. What is happening here – it comes as no surprise to the youth. At the same time there is always a chance – a possibility of something other. 'Adam said it was the most natural thing in the world, I seem to remember.'

'You set a lot of store by what he says, don't you?' Zibby says. 'Shall we look at some old footage now? And stop apologising, for heaven's sake. Everyone's different, that's all. You're probably going to be outstanding at – I don't know – chess, or needlepoint, or baking a Battenberg cake.'

'That's terrific –' Davy says. 'Do let me know if you manage to come up with anything else to add to the list.' Now they get dressed back to back in a hurry and in silence, this silence shaped by mixed manifestations of disappointment, resentment and relief. They are both thinking the same thing – it is hardly worth plugging the dinky little heater back in at this late stage in the proceedings.

CHAPTER TWENTY-ONE
Time Itself

DINNER IS OVER. IN THE BANQUETING SUITE at the Abercrombie Hotel, the Conservative Association members sit back, replete, and listen to the closing stages of an address by their new president, who stands at a centrally positioned table and speaks without notes.

'So, let me conclude, friends,' Saunders takes up, 'because I can see many of you are chomping on your cigars in anticipation of the toast, or thinking about squeezing back into your dancing pumps in the case of the ladies –' Murmurs of amused appreciation break out to left and right of the speaker. 'Let me conclude on a more personal note by telling you a story. I want to take you back more years than I care to number – to when I was a young lad growing up in British East Africa, at Mombasa on the coast, where we had a remarkable cook by the name of Ishmael.' As the president continues his address, Lydia James surveys the complacent faces of his attentive audience. What does she think? She thinks the man who speaks is worth all the rest put together. He is unlike these others. He is self-evidently the best of them – that is why he stands before them now. Lydia's feeling – it takes hold in a garden only recently penetrated by the sun. 'Well, Ishmael hailed from Somaliland –' Saunders advises, 'black as coal and, as I say, a first-rate cook. One afternoon as we played together on the beach after school, Ishmael said something that made a great impression on me. I suppose I had my eyes shut for the sake of the game as he poured the hot white sand into my cupped hands beside the Indian Ocean. Ishmael poured and poured, and to me it seemed that time itself was running though my fingers until, eventually, the pouring stopped and I opened my eyes. In my cupped hands I was holding the largest spider a boy could ever hope to set eyes on.' Here and there now a sharp intake of breath makes itself heard. 'Well, you can imagine my surprise.' Cue a ripple of laughter. 'I must admit to a sense of betrayal as I tossed the thing away. I imagine I was not a little shaken up. But the Somali appeared to think nothing of it. Just two words he uttered, ladies and gentlemen – two words intended to impart what he understood of life to me who knew next to nothing of it. Change coming, he said, and he left me sitting there on the hot sand. I wish I knew how he pulled off that trick, because three weeks later a certain archduke was assassinated in an obscure city here on the continent of Europe. The rest is, as we say, history. The point is that we are all a part of it, are we not? We shape it, even as it shapes us. We are each of us making history every day, in our own way, a little at a time, and our freedoms are bought by our actions –'

In the darkened playroom at the Saunders residence, flickering light picks out a gazelle's head on a plaque on the wall and an unidentified bird of prey that appears to hang suspended in mid-swoop from the ceiling. Zibby and Davy sit side by side in two large armchairs, their faces bathed in the patchy light as, from the table between them, its take-up spool clicking rhythmically, the projector throws a soundless black and white image jerkily at the screen. What do we see? We see the younger Zibby Saunders. Her features fill the frame, out of focus, far too close. First, she sticks her tongue out as if she knows we are watching, then she turns and flees. In a field surrounded by snow-

149

clad hills the villagers pull faces as they become aware of the roving camera. A mongrel dog cocks its leg against the wheel of a pram for the benefit of a newspaper man with a camera, but the reporter fails to notice the dog. That is because his attention is directed at a group of young men who pose, squinting and shielding their eyes from an unlikely sun, with their heavy prams in tow, beside what can best be described as a tennis umpire's high chair that dominates the scene. The sun withdraws. Pouf! The reporter's flashbulb goes off silently.

Now the young men on the screen prod their prams and inspect the wheels of their prams and blow into cupped hands and poke each other's chests and beat their arms to keep warm. Inside the prams sit the girls, their heads wrapped around with scarves or covered by balaclavas, their knees tucked up to their chins. As a light snow falls, the villagers grin and wave and form an avenue beyond the umpire's chair on the track that leads to the famous hill. Is that Lydia James we glimpse now behind the rope and beside a younger Adam Boyd? It could hardly be anyone else, could it? Oh, look – there goes little Davy James, stumbling about in a thicket of wellies. Adam turns to Lydia and whispers something in her ear, and Lydia laughs gaily as she shares with her part-time lover some insight destined to further their intimacy, or to betray it to anyone who happens to look on.

'Have we seen her yet?' Davy asks without taking his eyes off the screen. 'Or is she behind the camera? Your mother –'

'She's behind the camera,' Zibby says. 'I chose this one because I knew your mother was in it.' Here, she lights a cigarette and passes it through the beam to Davy, then lights one for herself. 'She looks happy, doesn't she?' she says. 'Your mother, I mean.' No reply from Davy seated beside her. 'What are you going to do?' she asks him at last. 'I'm not going to partner you,' she confirms after a while. 'Don't think I've changed my mind, Davy, because I haven't.'

'Aren't we going to see any footage of the race?' He is thinking about the images he has just viewed. He is not thinking of his mother and a young Adam Boyd. Instead, he pictures himself wheeling this way and that in a forest of adult legs. He is not running away from anything. He is running towards something – something akin to the truth, he decides, in so far as it has revealed itself to him at such a tender age. 'Aren't there any shots of the hill?'

'What difference does it make? Isn't it time you faced facts? As in – aren't you facing the prospect of having to withdraw from the whole shooting match? No partner, no race –'

'Those girls will need partners, won't they, come next weekend? Someone will have to pick me in the end. That's how it is. Someone is bound to partner me at the last minute.'

'I wouldn't bet on it. I honestly wouldn't –'

'I just want someone to choose me. Is that too much to ask, God-personage in the sky?'

'At least you've still got your fiver. Who needs partners or friends when you've got five quid in your pocket?'

On the screen, careering prams jostle for position and scramble for advantage in a chaotic first dash from the umpire's chair along a roped-off track lined for a short distance on both sides with partisan onlookers. Already the stricken chariots – one or two early casualties – sprawl here and there in the mud. The shrieks of the unseated girls are silent shrieks. Now the take-up spool turns more rapidly and the smoke from two cigarettes cavorts in the projector beam, but the film has run out and the viewing screen is bright with hot light.

A respectful silence reigns in the hotel's banqueting suite. Saunders pours himself more water from the jug. He smiles with good humour at the room before taking up again fluently and finally.

'In these uncertain times, my friends, when nationhood is called increasingly into question, it is to our higher selves and to each other that we look for a true sense of who we might best be, and what we might best become. Sometimes things happen to us, and sometimes we make things happen. Here, let me commend to you the selfless efforts of Martha Lees in raising the prize funds for next weekend's Scramble, which many believe will be our last.' Polite applause runs up and down the room accompanied by fulsome murmurs of *hear, hear*. 'Each of us,' Saunders says, 'is master of his fate. Each of us has something to give – for is that not the Conservative way? Every one of us has a part to play. Let us play it. And now –' As he raises and presents his brandy glass for the toast, the chairs shuffle backwards from the tables. Soon the room is on its feet. 'The Queen –' Saunders proposes, and all are in ready agreement with him.

CHAPTER TWENTY-TWO
Solid Air, Shifting Ground

THE ENGINE RUNS, THE HEATING IS ON. We are back inside his car. Lydia sits up front with Saunders in the Daimler Regency saloon as, outside and all around, departing vehicles crunch their way slowly across the gravel in the car park of the Abercrombie Hotel. The wind has died – now the temperature falls away. Beyond this steamed-up windscreen, headlights pierce the solid air above the lake with arrows of silver and gold.

'Are we, perhaps, making a habit of this?' Lydia asks Saunders after he presents her with a glass of champagne.

'Left-overs,' he informs her, 'from an ill-fated Christmas picnic.'

'Was it so ill-fated?' she says. 'It brought us to this place and this hour. Didn't someone once tell me we must learn to love the past?'

'Not at the expense of the present, surely –' Saunders suggests, contented but not complacent, as he tucks the champagne bottle into a pocket in the door beside him.

'I suppose we must pity the present,' Lydia says, her smile just visible to him behind her raised collar. 'Ever a poor relation to what goes before and what comes after.'

'Oh, I wouldn't necessarily go that far,' Saunders says, clinking his glass against Lydia's. 'The Queen –' he proposes for the second time tonight. 'While she remains young, beautiful and, yes, a *present*

153

inspiration to her people.' He sips to seal the toast. Lydia makes no move, as expected. He is waiting for her to return her glass with her customary and special look.

'I'm sure you were rather impressive tonight,' she says, eyes cast down decently in a measured response to the absurd compliment he pays her. When she gives him back her glass it is understood between them – this is exactly how life unfolds in a steamed-up car in a near empty car park on a frosty night in the run-up to Christmas. 'Yes –' she concludes. 'We are definitely making a habit of this.'

'I can think of worse habits,' Saunders says, draining both glasses before passing them to Lydia. 'Shall I take you home now, perhaps?'

Fifteen minutes later the Daimler draws up outside the old stone house on the northern shore of the lake. The house is in darkness – there is only the solitary street lamp that stands guard crookedly a short distance away. Saunders switches off headlights and engine.

'Why should you be alone tonight?' he asks Lydia.

'Tonight,' she tells him, 'is not the night.'

'I'm asking you,' he says, 'to make a choice.'

'I suppose,' she says, 'we must be most like ourselves in the dark.'

'I'm asking you to choose, Lydia,' he says.

'And that is what I am doing,' she tells him. She passes him one of the glasses she has been holding since they quit the hotel car park, then opens the car door a little. 'Thank you for a wonderful evening,' she says as if she has weighed each word with great care. 'I was about to thank you for a memorable evening, but that would sound formal or cold, even though it's a true enough reflection. You have opened a window on the world – just as you promised to.' Then it occurs to her – until quite recently she might have said *just as you threatened to*. Now everything has changed. 'I don't mean you promised to open a window on the world in that sense,' she goes on. 'I am not speaking of Sarajevo, say, or Mombasa beside the sea.' Here, she hands him the second of the two glasses she has been holding. 'And we will see each other again very soon, won't we?'

He watches her all the way to the front door. As she reaches the step, he sees it – he sees the curtain move slightly at the bay window facing the lake. That is strange, he thinks. Is Davy at home with the place in darkness? He would have expected the son of the house to be elsewhere still in the company of one Zibby Saunders. Is it late? As he drives back towards the village, Saunders can see the lights of Müller's Christmas tree on the southern shore of the lake. It may be late, he tells himself, but it can't be that late.

Lydia enters the room, switches on the light, stops. Adam Boyd sits in an armchair turned away from the fireplace towards the door. He has a bottle of what looks like whisky in his hand. He gets up, walks to the window, and turns on the lights at the tree. 'Merry Christmas,' he says, raising the bottle in a toast to the past, or to who knows what.

She is standing beside the door still. As she takes off her coat, she realises with a mental shrug she is without her gloves – the ones that today carry a small cigarette burn if you know where to look. She is thinking about what it all means. Adam's presence here tonight – it is just another part of the voyage, isn't it? Then it comes to Lydia – she has not yet reached the other side. Not quite.

Now Adam indicates the paraffin heater, which is lit and giving out its aroma. 'I took the liberty,' he says. Another swig here from a near empty bottle. 'Nice motor,' he tells Lydia. 'Very nice motor –'

'It's late, Adam, and I'm tired. What do you want?'

'I was thinking we must be at least half way to the next full moon. I was thinking you might be lonely at such a time – the way you used to be. I was thinking about how the roof might need fixing again. I

155

was thinking about how we might spend more time together now in this house. I mean as a family. Where is the lad, anyway?'

'Out,' she says.

'I got to thinking this might be his night for practising The Holly And The Ivy with his friends from the choir.'

'Not tonight,' Lydia says, closing the door and dropping her coat and stole onto a chair.

'Must be a confusing time for the boy,' Adam says. 'Could be he wishes he had never discovered who is real father is, or was, or will be. Could be he wishes things had stayed the way they were. Maybe it would have been better if they had.'

Is she ready for this? Indeed, she is – she has rehearsed the whole thing a thousand times in her head. 'I don't hold with that view,' she tells Adam now. 'And neither do you. Rather the inconvenient truth than an endless lie –'

'In that case, maybe we should go one further. Maybe we should be sharing with the world the happy news about Davy's parentage.'

'Is that in Davy's interest? I mean at this time?'

'When would the right time be, Lydia? Aren't you the expert in these things?'

'Perhaps when you've decided what kind of father you want to be to him.'

'I don't know the answer to that one. Perhaps I don't want to be known as his father at all. Did you consider that when you decided to swap a fifteen-year-old lie for the truth – a truth with no need of itself, a reality with no proper reason to exist? Davy is not like other boys. How can you be sure he's my boy, for that matter? He doesn't even look like me.'

'Davy is your son, Adam. What you choose to make of that is up to you at all times and in all weathers.'

'He is not like other sons.'

'What do you mean by that?'

'You know what I mean.'

'Go home now, please. You're drunk. Might I suggest you think about what is best for the boy, not yourself? You speak of the truth. It's true that Davy must take ownership of his body, as we all must. And he will find his own way. But I repeat – Davy is your son.'

'The boy is not made like me.'

'How exactly are you made, Adam? What type of man are you really? I'm not sure any of us knows. I'm not sure you know yourself. Perhaps this is your chance to find out –'

The sound of a vehicle pulling up outside the house. She knows who it is. So does Adam. From the bay window she sees Saunders and Davy get out of the car. Davy's bike protrudes from the boot of the Daimler. 'Go now, please,' she tells Adam.

'I am not ashamed,' he says, 'of who I am.'

Now Saunders and Davy are inside the house. As Davy climbs the stairs rapidly, the living room door opens to admit Saunders. In his hand he carries Lydia's gloves. 'You left these in the car,' he says from the doorway.

'Thank you,' she says. 'I believe Adam is just leaving.'

'Good night, Lydia,' Adam says. As he passes her, he opens her hand and presses it inside – the locket she gave him all those winters ago. At the door he takes the bottle from under his arm and thrusts it at Saunders without otherwise acknowledging his presence. Then he is gone, and a silence descends.

'Did you leave your gloves behind deliberately so that I would have to return them?'

'That would be quite something, wouldn't it? Did you hide them on purpose to give yourself an excuse to come back here?'

'That would be quite something, wouldn't it? I saw the curtain move earlier, and then I met Davy coming home on his bike. Stands to reason there was someone here with you.'

'And you wanted to know who that someone was?'

'You should lock your doors. It could have been anyone.'

'That's true,' Lydia says, turning down a chance here to explain that Adam Boyd holds, has always held, a key to this house. 'Thank you again. Once upon a time I seemed to do nothing but apologise to you. Now I do little else but thank you, it seems.'

'Is everything all right here?' Saunders asks.

'Yes,' she says.

'Are you sure? You don't want me to stay for a while?'

'I don't think that would be right, do you? I've had quite enough excitement for one night, I do believe. Didn't I say it not half an hour ago? We'll see each other again soon.'

'As you wish,' Saunders says. He is preparing to leave the room and the house when he thinks of something. No – something comes back to him as if it has been waiting in the wings. 'There's something you should know,' he says from the doorway.

'Oh?' she says. She is very tired now, and there is so much novel information about life to process or digest. It comes to her in a cold rush – this idea that her encounter with Adam tonight might be seen by the world as something planned. That is too much, she thinks.

Then Saunders steps inside the room again and closes the door behind him. The man of the world is also a bank manager, after all. 'Davy's school bursary –' he says. 'You should know that these funds are made available on a charitable basis by Mr Murphy. That's right – old man Murphy is your benefactor in this regard. Of course, it's a private matter, a confidential matter, as you'd expect. But I want there to be no secrets between us from now on. Do you understand what I'm telling you, Lydia? I know Murphy would see it in the same way. Murphy is nobody's fool. Some things are more important than money, he would say. Loyalty and truth – these are relative values, and at any time this one may be worth more than that one.' Abruptly he is gone. Adam's bottle – he must add it to his collection, it seems. He won't wait for the woman of the house to come back to him. She has had quite enough excitement for one night, hasn't she?

At last she is alone. 'Thank you,' she whispers to an empty room. After she turns off the heater and the lights at the tree, she opens one curtain and peers at the lake. In the middle distance, a fox wheels in territorial loops, as if to vouchsafe the circumference of freedom on shifting ground. One day it will be over, Lydia tells herself, and the ice will go from the lake. For tonight, she is alone with her son in this austere but noble house, and that is good. That is all right. And, yes, in her hand she holds the locket that Adam has given back to her. In just a few minutes she will add this to the cache of beautiful relics she keeps in the mother-of-pearl box on the dressing table upstairs.

CHAPTER TWENTY-THREE
Being and Nothingness

THE DAY OF THE SCRAMBLE DAWNS COLD and clear. The sun has
not yet crested the eastern ridges, but already the brawny farmhands
are busy setting up in a field beside the muddy track that leads to the
famous hill at the back of the village. There is the marquee to erect,
and the first segment of the race route must be marked out with rope
slung between low posts behind which the spectators will gather. It
is no easy task to sink these posts into the hard ground – at two or
three second intervals the mallet blows ring out, bouncing back off
the hillside and scouring the village streets before rolling out across
the lake and dying on the far shoreline. A horsebox draws up on the
road at the edge of the field – Murphy's field – where the marquee
is spread out on the turf in a large rectangle attended by farmhands
with guy ropes at the ready. Jumping down now from the horsebox
on the passenger side with a megaphone in his hand is Lees, cheating
husband of nice Mrs Lees. The PE instructor has what looks to be a
prime managerial role here – certainly he takes a step backwards as
the rear of the horsebox comes clattering down like a drawbridge at
the practised hands of the driver. Soon they are all at it. One by one
the battered prams roll down the slope from horsebox to field. These
war-worn chariots have many a tale to tell of secret hopes and public
humiliations, of personal battles won and lost in the Christmas mud

160

and the rain. For now, they look a sorry sight, rounded up like cattle for the slaughter and left to reflect on being and nothingness in an icy corner of Murphy's field. At a key point in the proceedings, Lees raises his megaphone and does what he has been looking forward to doing for the past one and a half hours.

Testing, testing – one, two, three.

On the count of three, Davy James wakes up in his bedroom in the old stone house on the far shore of the lake. In fact, he has only recently fallen asleep, having spent a large part of the night thinking about it all. He is thinking about what is going to happen. Today is a big day, he tells himself, staring at the ceiling with his hands behind his head. Normally at this time on Sunday morning he would clean out the fireplace in the room below and then offer to discharge any other domestic tasks such as are necessary before getting dressed for church. Today, however, is not a day for sermon or songbook. That is what the youth has concluded at some stage during the long, lonely night. Davy's mother will today attend church without him, and in the choir stalls beside Mrs Lees a vacant place will make itself known to anyone who has an eye for these things.

In the field behind the village, the preparations continue without let-up. Now three or four resourceful farmhands haul an outlandish wooden form from the depths of the horsebox. Standing upright in short order is what can only be described as a high chair of the type favoured by tennis umpires at the better class of tournament.

'You beauty –' Lees says, eyeing the structure fondly with head tilted this way and that and deploying the megaphone again for good measure. 'You absolute beauty.'

A Daimler Regency saloon draws up outside the old stone house in which Davy James lives with his mother, Lydia. The car horn sounds twice in a relaxed manner. Zibby Saunders gets out on the passenger side, half-closes the car door, and approaches the front door of the house with her cine camera swinging from her wrist on a short strap. Before Zibby gets a chance to knock, the door opens to reveal Davy's mother. Lydia stands in the hall at the bottom of the stairs, pulling on her gloves in front of an oval mirror that hangs above the console table and beside a hat stand that harbours a selection of umbrellas.

'Don't bother asking what I think about the whole thing, Zibby,' Lydia says, adjusting her scarlet beret in the mirror. 'No partner, no race. I mean – what could be simpler or more clear-cut?'

'Where is he?' Zibby demands.

'Upstairs,' Lydia tells her. 'But don't waste your breath.'

'Let me speak to him,' Zibby says, squeezing past Lydia and then racing up the stairs. Left, or right? On the landing she doesn't know which way to turn. 'Davy?' she calls out.

'What do *you* want?' he calls out after a second or two.

At first, she stands in the doorway at a decent remove. Then she remembers – not so long ago they confronted each other naked on a mattress. 'What's going on?' she asks.

'Nothing's going on,' Davy says, rolling away towards the wall.

Now she perches on the edge of his bed like a big sister. 'Are you coming, or aren't you?'

'Maybe yes, maybe no,' he says in a way which strikes Zibby as childish but which sums up his ambivalence in the face of everything available for consideration at this time.

'Come on, then,' she says. 'We don't have all bloody day.'

'What's the great rush? Might as well hang fire to see if there's any stragglers left after everyone registers.'

Now she can see it – he hasn't moved on. He is stuck in exactly the same position as he occupied before. She had imagined he would come to terms with himself and the world, or the way the world goes about its ugly business, at the last. But no – he is stuck. 'Grow up, Davy –' she says. 'It's only a stupid pram race.'

'Is it?' Davy says. 'Adam Boyd called it a scramble for something lost that can never be found. In other words, it had meaning for him. He scoffs at it, but it still means something to him. What do you think of that, Elvis-the-Pelvis? Put that in your pipe and smoke it.'

In the car, Lydia sits up front beside Saunders. Behind these two, Zibby breathes on the lens of her camera and wipes it carefully with the sleeve of her cardigan. 'I think he must be trying to make me feel guilty for holding out against him,' she announces now.

'He's just disappointed,' Lydia insists brightly. Even as she issues this utterly conventional verdict on her son's state of mind, she sees her words reach backwards and forwards to embrace the beginning and the end of the affair – yes, of everything – as he sees it. She is moved by this modest familial revelation. Meanwhile, the car makes slow progress. That is because the way is blocked time and again by groups of villagers heading, all of them, in the same direction. Lydia looks at Saunders, or, rather, she looks *for* the man beside her, the man who would put an end to secrets by sharing them. Yesterday, or the day before, she didn't know. She had no inkling of the reality. Today, she knows that Davy's bursary benefactor is none other than Murphy, a man she has always despised and dismissed without ever understanding why. If she has been wrong-footed by the facts, she doesn't care. She has no plans to lodge an appeal. If she finds herself on the wrong side of the argument or the truth, she doesn't blame the man who sits beside her. This man will always know what to do, Lydia tells herself. This man will always see things for what they are. 'Would you mind terribly taking me home?' she asks him calmly and quietly. 'I'm awfully sorry – I think I should go back home.'

Then Saunders turns towards her and shakes his head. 'I think,' he says, 'we should probably all do our best to leave the young man alone now, don't you?'

By the time they reach the field behind the village, the marquee is already full of bodies keeping warm, or trying to keep warm. There are no organised refreshments as such. Instead, a variety of flasks of the thermos and hip variety do the rounds according to local custom. There is much stamping of boots on the wooden duckboards. The atmosphere is suitably expectant, the air thick with smoke. Oh, look – Betty from the Post Office rises up on tip-toe and waves her cheery greeting through the festive fog. 'Shall we go inside for a spell,' Lydia says, 'before the whole thing kicks off?'

'You go in with Zibby,' Saunders says. 'I think I'll have a little look around first.'

'If there's any looking around to be done,' Zibby puts in, holding her camera up for inspection, 'it's probably me that should do it.'

Sitting behind a trestle table parked to one side of the marquee, Lees writes carefully in a ledger, tongue protruding slightly through his teeth, as, on the other side of the table, a gaggle of mostly youths gathers to register, or re-register, for today's big event. 'Name?' Lees says. He waits, pen poised, without looking up. 'Name?' The familiar giggle goes out, followed by the familiar snigger. When Lees glances up finally, he finds himself confronted by Murdo and Erica, arm in arm or hand in hand.

'OK, you two lovebirds – what's so funny today?'

'Nothing, sir,' Erica says. 'I thought you would have known our names by now, that's all.'

'Corporal McLean reporting for duty, sir. Please, sir – is it true what they say, sir?'

'What exactly do they say, Murdo?'

164

'Is it true you shagged one of the kitchen maids at school on the floor of the walk-in pantry, sir? You know the one, sir – the blonde skivvy who looks about sixteen, going on fifteen and a half.'

Just out of earshot here, nice Mrs Lees paces up and down at the base of the umpire's chair. She wears her Sunday best coat and hat above a pair of stout shoes for which the term sensible was probably invented by people who know about these things. Mrs Lees positions a megaphone in front of her face and practises as quietly as she can, directing her efforts towards the famous hill and generally away from the tent, the tent from which villagers and visitors are increasingly spilling out in anticipation of the race. 'Mayday, mayday –' Mrs Lees whispers, this signal going out to anyone who has an ear for it.

Inside the packed marquee, Betty and Lydia chat fluently, freely, as if chatting itself might one day go out of fashion, or end up being rationed by court injunction, while Zibby functions as best she can in the limited space available for documentary filmmaking. 'Forty-nine?' Betty hazards. 'Fifty, perhaps, at a push?'

'Why don't you just ask him?' Lydia says, grateful for a chance to laugh.

'What? You mean you don't even know how old he is, chuck?'

Then the focus of their dialogue joins them carrying two cups of something hot – one cup with, and one without, sugar, as he advises. 'No sign –' Saunders says for Lydia's benefit, shaking his head. 'I've just had a quiet word with Lees.'

'I had reason to believe my only begotten son had put his name down for today's fun and games,' Lydia explains for Betty's sake.

'Who? Davy? I don't think so –'

Now the Jamieson spinsters heave into view alongside them like imperial swans, matching tea cups at the ready, the crowd parting like the Red Sea before them as they glide and nod. 'A small sherry is very pleasant, my dear,' admits the first Miss Jamieson, her gloved fingers on Lydia's arm.

'A small sherry is most welcome,' says the second Miss Jamieson. 'Especially as this might be our last Scramble. I imagine young Davy will want to be here to witness a bit of history in the making.'

'Marvellous singing voice, my dear,' says the first Miss Jamieson, withdrawing smoothly as if on well-oiled and highly-geared wheels, her sibling companion in tow.

'Steady as she goes, ladies,' Saunders urges on behalf of the local community.

Then it begins. From somewhere beyond these tented walls they hear the random squawk of a loud hailer as Lees prepares to call the meeting to order. Immediately, the hubbub inside the marquee goes up a few notches in pitch and volume.

'Here we go,' Betty says to Lydia.

'Where's Zibby?' Lydia says to Saunders.

'Taking up position with her camera, I should think.'

'When you're ready, good people —' Lees booms for all to hear. 'We have a starter's orders situation brewing, if I'm not mistaken.'

'Will you be all right?' Saunders asks Lydia, squeezing her hand.

'Of course,' she tells him. 'Let's get it over with, shall we?'

CHAPTER TWENTY-FOUR
The Gala Day

ON EITHER SIDE OF THE TRACK THE SPECTATORS take up position, assembling one or two-deep behind the rope and as close as they can get to the starting line, which is also the finishing line. From the start line, above which the high chair rises like an instrument of torture, the muddy track leads only to the infamous hill. This hill, which is, strictly speaking, a hillock or a mound dominated from behind by much larger and more impressive geological features, the competing pram teams must both ascend and descend during the next half hour in an all-out race against each other and employing such tactics as may be necessary to impede, slow, or cancel altogether the progress of their rivals. Nobody knows how it started. Nobody knows why or when. No one can recall a time when there wasn't a Scramble. The more absurd or arcane the ritual, the readier we are as a community to uphold it and honour it, or to defend its right to exist. This is our country – the best country in the world.

Below the umpire's chair and behind the start line, some thirty contestants – the pick, by and large, of our younger adults for miles around – await with their prams the arrival of the starter, in pairs of male and female, their focus at this time on padding the interiors of their chariots, or surveying the lie of the land ahead in terms of the softness or firmness of the going underfoot, or exchanging low-level

167

insults and ribald remarks with their rivals, or making their partisan case for occupying the coveted front rank when the balloon goes up, this question of the rankings decided quite properly by age, with the youngest males lining up first on the grid. Coming and going around the domain of prams are the newsmen with their notebooks, and two or three official snappers with loaded devices. Zibby Saunders is in there too, of course – she finds her softly whirring camera creates, when raised to the eye and actively engaged, an ideal relationship between subject and documentarist, so that she is at once connected to, and insulated from, the wicked world. In Zibby's sights right now are prominent classmates Ted and Janice, the one tucked up snugly inside their chosen chariot of destiny, the other lashing out at a pram wheel with his boot in the hope of achieving an enhanced alignment before the whistle blows and the magpies scatter. Now we are in the company of Murdo and Erica – impossible to overlook these darlings with their noses poking out from makeshift balaclavas. Erica raises a hip flask in a tipsy toast for the sake of Zibby's all-seeing camera, while Murdo uncovers his best leer in a nod to posterity. 'Could have been you, baby,' he reminds Zibby with a wink.

Fifty yards up the track from the start line, Saunders joins Lydia and Betty behind the rope, the spaces around them filling up rapidly with spectators. Lydia can't help it – every so often she leans forward over the rope and peers to left and right along the track. What is she looking for? She hardly knows. Whatever it is, it fills her with a kind of horror or dread.

'I'm sure he's got far better things to do with his time,' Betty tells Saunders. 'Wise young man, if you want my opinion –'

Enthroned finally on the high chair above the start line, nice Mrs Lees, official race starter, gazes down fondly on the younger children gathering noisily just below her sensible shoes. In her lap she has the giant handbag entrusted by tradition with an important role. In her hand she holds a scribbled speech. Now she accepts the megaphone from her cheating spouse and clears her throat as the flashbulbs pop redundantly in the watery sunshine.

'My lords, ladies and gentlemen —' A ripple of what sounds like humorous indulgence runs along the ropes on either side of the track as our audience searches in vain for a lord. As she waits patiently for quiet, Mrs Lees shushes the little ones below. 'It is indeed a privilege to be asked once again to preside —' At this point a heckler interrupts mischievously to enquire *who asked?* 'To preside,' the starter takes up, 'over these proceedings, which have a tradition stretching back more than half a century —' *So, proceed, woman, proceed.* Mrs Lees looks down at her spouse. She is on the verge of some private anguish. After her spouse signals at her to get a move on, Mrs Lees abandons her notes. 'This year once again, the Scramble prize fund stands at fifty pounds to be shared by the winning couple. Good luck. God speed —'

She has surrendered the hailer to Lees and, with it, her moral authority as race starter. Funny – she has never been heckled before. Is it a sign of the times? This is hardly the moment to speculate, Mrs Lees tells herself. The giant handbag has not yet discharged its role. As the little ones await the important business of the handbag, the prams behind them begin their ultimate jostling, and Lees points the iconic megaphone at the sky.

On your marks —

Among the spectators gathered behind the rope at the furthest remove from the umpire's chair there is a small commotion. Heads are already turning away from the muddy track to take in some new visual interest or experience. The first whoops and wolf-whistles can be heard at this time. It behoves the replacement starter, however, to continue with his historic countdown.

169

Get set –

When Lees looks up at his wife, he sees her hug the vast handbag protectively to her bosom. What can it be that distracts her so at this key moment? Lees cannot see what is happening. He is aware of the commotion, but he can't see anything. When he steps forward from behind the high chair he sees a lone figure in the middle of the track at a distance of fifty or sixty yards. There is a great deal of jeering and catcalling now from behind the ropes on both sides.

Davy James stands in the middle of the muddy track and shivers. Above his mother's sling back shoes he wears a summer skirt with a pretty floral pattern – a favourite of his, of course – and a turquoise blouse that is new to him. His lipstick is cherry red. His earrings are of the shiny drop variety. But what is he cradling in those bare arms? Oh, I say – he's only gone and brought the one-armed Jesus doll, rescued from the frozen surface of the lake and complete with tatty tinsel crown, along with him today for support and good measure.

Now Lydia James starts forward from behind the barrier, but in this she finds herself impeded by Saunders and his ally, Betty. 'Get off me,' Lydia protests, but it does no good. Those who restrain her are bent on denying her access to her son, despite her distress.

Meanwhile, Davy sets off slowly, his advance shaped by rutted mud, towards the start line and the prams and the chair and the kids. The din is incredible now – cheers mix with jeers against a backdrop of hoots and whistles. Within seconds Zibby gets in on the act – she walks backwards in front of Davy with her camera on the youth and the enduring hills behind his head. When he reaches the starting line and the umpire's chair, Davy wrests the loud hailer from a surprised replacement starter after a brief tug-of-war which can only have one winner. As Davy raises the hailer up, the noise dies away completely. Fitting, somehow, that Lees is left holding the dolly of transgression in the deepening silence. You could probably hear a pin drop during this interlude in Murphy's crusty field at the back of our fair village.

'I am looking,' Davy begins rather unsteadily, 'for a partner for this year's Scramble. I mean any partner. I don't care who it is. I'm really not fussed. I don't care what this partner looks like. Except, of course, it's going to have to be a bloke now.' After a lone wolf-whistle goes out, the profound silence returns. 'Like I say, I'm not bothered. Any geezer will do – just as long as he's made of the right stuff. So, let's be having you, gents. Step right up, and let's see how good you really are. Handsome prizes to be won here, and history to be made.'

Now it is almost finished. Adam Boyd steps over the rope a short distance from the start line and makes his way calmly towards our young speaker. Will he be in time? He had better hurry if he wants to get there in time. 'Don't be shy, chaps,' Davy says, voice faltering, 'because anyone can score today.' Then Adam's coat comes off and the megaphone takes a tumble and Davy falls into Adam's arms, or, rather, into his big warm coat, and Adam bears him off through the prams. Now Lees scoops up the megaphone and casts off the horrid doll and does his civic duty on this gala day in late December as the first rumours of serious misconduct swirl around his head.

Go, go, go –

Mrs Lees upends her huge handbag. A shower of coins of mostly smaller denominations rains down on the muddy track just in front of the start line. As the little ones scramble, shrieking and hollering, for the treasure, the impudent prams force their way into the picture, trampling tiny fingers under their wheels and heading for the hills in search of the thing that can never be found. When he thinks back on this last Scramble, Davy recalls only the most random and obscure details – Zibby's hand beckoning him forward towards her camera on the avenue of shame, and a lone osprey hanging, muscular wings

171

extended, in a shaft of thicker air above the unseen lake. Oh – and Adam's big warm coat. Davy remembers that much.

Behind the rope that lines the track, Betty withdraws discreetly as Saunders fetches Lydia closer. He doesn't apologise for holding her back just a few moments ago, nor would she expect or want him to. 'If there are to be no secrets between us from now on,' Lydia says, 'then there is something I must tell you about Davy's father.'

'Ah,' Saunders says. 'I have a feeling I know what you're about to say. But tell me anyway –'

Zibby will have to get home under her own steam. On the way back in the car they pass Adam and Davy wheeling Davy's bike at the side of the road, but instead of stopping they sail straight on with only a honk of acknowledgement. Lydia doesn't say anything. More and more she elects to follow the Saunders method and mode. More and more she relies on the bank manager's judgement and instinct.

'Your house or my house?' he asks with his signature insight and subtlety, his enquiry taking in every facet of the current case as seen from every point of view.

'Oh, yours,' Lydia says with only the slightest hesitation. 'I think that's probably best under the circumstances, don't you? At least for a short time until the dust settles.'

&⤳⤳

The ice has gone from the lake. We wait months for it to depart, and when it finally packs up and quits within forty-eight hours it's as if it has never been there at all. Why can't we let go?

Everything comes around. Old man Murphy flogs his land, and the surveyors arrive from Sheffield or Leeds, and, Bob's your uncle, they start building holiday homes – chalets, Murphy calls them – like there's no tomorrow. Only, there is – there is always tomorrow. It's here with us now. We worship God, some of us. We swim, those of us who can, in the lake, up until late September. Soon Müller's lights will make their welcome return to the lawn outside the Abercrombie Hotel. One day Davy may choose to sing again. Everything changes, but everything stays the same. That is OK with Davy James, at least for now, or until the dust settles on the current case. That is all right with me, at least for tonight, or until the sun comes up on a dream for the final time, and the meaning of the deer – the deer singular or plural – makes itself known to me at last.

EPILOGUE

Glasgow, December 1965

THE CITY, WHICH HAD A HARD-WON REPUTATION for squalor and violent crime, extended to me a warm enough welcome. They had warned me this place had heart. I didn't, or don't, know about that. I only know that to trade the brittle hospitality of Edinburgh, or the numbing chill that creeps in off the North Sea there, for the soft and penetrating drizzle that advances up Renfield Street from the Clyde was an unscheduled relief to me. At Queen Street station the carol singers were out in force. In George Square a Salvation Army band drew a small crowd to the base of a large Christmas tree – the gift, I conjectured, of a Scandinavian town in recognition of some extreme sacrifice or solidarity dating back to the war. All the starlings were shitting freely on the buildings around the square, on their blackened fronts, and no one seemed to mind. I limped freely on the wet streets of Glasgow. I mean I felt free to drag my leg around that city tough and tender – no one seemed to notice or care.

The bookshop was on Buchanan Street near the junction with St Vincent Place. Certain topographical details of my visit stand out – because I had no map of the city I was obliged to rely for directions on the kindness of strangers. And I was alone in Glasgow that day. My publisher's factotum, a charming but perennially sickly intern better suited to more temperate climes at, or around, the Tropic of

174

Kensington, languished with all expenses paid in a tartan-carpeted hotel in the draughty capital on the other side of Scotland. I had no plans to rescue her.

After lunching lightly and without benefit of an expense account at a Wimpy Bar on Union Street I presented myself a little early and took my seat behind the table set aside for me at the back of the shop. As soon as I sat down a short queue formed, and for the next fifteen minutes or so I was kept busy signing hardback copies of my book – a slight novel or, more properly, a novella set in a thickly veiled Soho of queer loyalties and unconventional morality – and penning words of dedication and seasonal goodwill on the title papers as instructed. Such engagement work I take very seriously. As might be expected, there were comparatively few takers for my book that afternoon in the city of persistent rain. I was on the point of bailing out, of cutting my losses and making directly for the London train, when it unfolded as if in a dream or a film. The young policeman ambled towards me from the front of the shop with a book – my book – held out rather stiffly in front of him. It was only when he took off his peaked cap – from the absence of a helmet I inferred, rightly or wrongly, he was some kind of officer or detective – that I saw it was Davy. Yes, the real Davy James was standing across the table from me with my book in his hand. He looked much the same – a little broader in the chest, perhaps, as a result of all those push-ups or pull-ups they would have made him do as a trainee or cadet. His thin moustache was designed, I imagined, to make him look older at the moment of apprehension or arrest in this or that suburb of the city. I had a strong urge, which I resisted, to jump up and embrace him. It occurred to me I would have subjected myself willingly to arrest by this particular lawman in any suburb or city you care to mention. When he smiled at me with maximum shyness it nearly broke my heart.

'Would you like me to dedicate it to someone special?' I asked rather wildly, opening the book and discovering inside it a scrap of paper with an address and a sketch map.

'To Davy is fine,' he said. 'Will you come to supper this evening at six o'clock?'

I took the electric train from Queen Street, alighting at Shettleston and covering the remainder of the ground on foot with the smell of coal fires and some factory discharge in the air around me. No pain is associated with my limp – I mean no physical pain. It just takes me a bit longer to get from A to B than it might take you. The house was a semi-detached affair on an estate of identical dwellings, their exteriors clad dismally using metal sheets that had been roughcast and painted grey, their gardens hemmed around by neatly trimmed hedges that rose to shoulder height. The neighbourhood in which my erstwhile Latin pupil lived was poor but decent – that is about the size and strength of it.

When a hall light came on and the front door opened, I got my first shock – no, my first surprise – of the evening. Davy's pretty wife introduced herself brightly, and welcomed me warmly inside their house. It wasn't long before I got my second surprise – or was it my second and third rolled into one? The older child, a toddler with a runny nose, peeked out from behind his father in the doorway to the living room. I know very little of these things, but I would have put the boy's age at three or four. The second child, a girl as I found out, was sucking on a bottle in Davy's arms. All this was utterly normal. At the same time, it was like a play staged by Davy for my benefit – within fifteen seconds of arriving I knew everything I needed to know about the young man's life. He wanted me to register everything. He wanted the world to know what had become of him, and what he had quietly and happily become. That is what I would tell you if you asked me to describe how things were in that tidy hallway in a poor but decent suburb of Glasgow in the December of 1965.

Part of me wants to forget the evening – I write this much down here, tonight, in the interests of completeness only. We ate luncheon meat fritters with peas, and, of course, Davy asked me what I knew of the fair village we had both left behind. What is there to tell? Old man Murphy passed away peacefully and was buried with fanfare in the overspill cemetery not far from the lake. Murdo McLean did a stretch for aggravated assault at a detention centre in Carlisle. Before Mrs Lees sued for divorce her cheating husband served a longer spell for something more serious at a secure facility somewhere close to Blackpool and the sea. As far as I knew, Adam Boyd was still living in a chalet bequeathed to him by Murphy in recognition of services to the family estate. When I asked Davy about his father, he said he had lost touch with Adam after moving to Glasgow to begin a new life there. After he learned I was living and working in London, Davy told me I should look up his mother, married now to the former bank manager, of course. I have no plans to look up Lydia any time soon. As for Zibby Saunders in America – it seems unlikely I'll be boarding that big silver bird, destination San Francisco, in the near future.

Just before I left to return to my hotel in the city, Davy asked me politely about my writing. I told him that the tale he had in mind – our tale, or, more accurately, his tale – was now in development at the BBC as a one-hour regional television drama with all the names changed. This was only a part of the thing. In fact, the same story had also been optioned as a feature film script by an independent production company in London. I didn't mention that bit to Davy. When he asked me what he should look out for in terms of a project title I said I didn't know. This was a white lie. The truth is I couldn't bring myself to dredge up those hysterical rantings about a lake and some deer. To try to explain all that – it wouldn't have been fair on the mother of Davy's children, quite apart from anything else.

At the front door we were alone together for the first time that evening, and the last time in general. Davy handed me a book that he must have put aside earlier with just this scene in mind. The book was the copy of Kennedy's Revised Latin Primer I had given him almost ten years ago in the old stone house on the northern shore of the lake. When I opened the battered volume, I saw an inscription written in ink in Davy's best hand.

> *Like icebergs in a tropic sea,*
> *Like moose's antlers on a flea,*
> *Like salt and salad cream with tea,*
> *Are adjectives that don't agree.*

Of course, I gave the book straight back to Davy on the doorstep of his house in Glasgow. I really had no need of it any more. And Davy must have known I would return it in a kind of formal rejection of the past. He put the book down and took up a small paper parcel and pressed it into my hand and asked me not to open it until I was over the hill and far away. On the empty train back to the city I tore open my parcel and there it was – the monogrammed handkerchief I had forced Davy to accept half a lifetime ago at the edge of a frozen lake as the blood from his nose merged with the down on his upper lip. Naturally, the bloodstained accessory had been washed and then ironed to within an inch of its laundered life before being put away in the bottom drawer of a tallboy, and, in my heart of hearts, I knew these to be the carefully considered actions of the young Davy James. For the record, there was a note inserted into the handkerchief – just two words written in large capitals on a blue sheet torn from a letter writing pad and folded over a couple of times – although it was hard to know at this distance exactly why I was being thanked.

It had stopped raining finally. Outside the station the Sally Army band had long since packed up – now the brooding square was given over to a handful of singing drunks and a matching tally of pigeons roosting, their heads tucked in tightly, on the monumental lions in front of the cenotaph. There was the illuminated Christmas tree, of course, which took me straight back, as such a tree always will, to Müller's famous lights outside the Abercrombie Hotel. Were they, perhaps, twinkling still – tonight – those lovely lights, beside the iced-up lake? I really wanted to think so. When I got to my room I sat on the bed with my wet coat on and set down these last few pages. Then it was over. For the first time in many a moon I slept the honest sleep of the young and the very good – there were no dreams, no Davys, and no deer. In accounting for my role in these historical events I have tried at all times to be true, old-fashioned as it may seem. To me this is wholly a matter of personal vanity and professional self-interest. Who speaks the truth can never be wrong.